BENEATH THESE BRIGHT STARS

WARDHAM BOOK 8

ZOE YORK

ZOYO PRESS

DEDICATION

that extra-sweet happiness a second chance brings

For Andrea, who wanted more

ABOUT THIS BOOK

You're invited to a very special Wardham wedding…

It's been a year since Liam and Evie welcomed their daughter Ava to the world. A year of sleepless nights and laughter-filled days. Some fights. A lot of love. And non-stop parenting. Plus they had a wedding to plan.

But now it's their time, and Liam wants to make the most of it.

Liam has never had any problem showing Evie how much he loves her, and now that they're making the ultimate commitment to each other, he wants to find exactly the right words as well. Then he'll go back to showing her, over and over again.

———

1

T HE clap of the back door swinging open caught Liam's attention and he spun around. He'd been outside in the late January cold with his soon-to-be stepsons for half an hour, and the afternoon light was fading, but the sight of his two beaming girls renewed his enthusiasm for backyard sledding.

His baby girl, and his fiancée, who would be his wife in nineteen days—a union more than a year overdue, but his bride wouldn't be rushed. She'd done it all once before, and this time, she said she wanted to get it right.

Looking at her proudly presenting their toddler in her puffy, pink parka, Liam wanted to remind her again for the umpteenth time that there was no way they could it get wrong, but it would just fall on deaf ears.

"Ava loves her new snowsuit," Evie said, beaming. "We thought we'd join you guys!"

His daughter didn't look quite as enthusiastic as her mother about this plan, but that was probably par for the course for one-year-olds. And her brothers were having a blast, sliding down the small hill at the back of their property.

He slid his gaze over Evie's own snowboard pants. "And if you have to go down on the sled with her?"

Evie winked. "The sacrifices I make for my children, right?"

He chuckled as they came close enough for kisses. "Never change. You're perfect."

"You're not going to say that after I tell you I've changed my mind on table centrepieces again. I've got some pictures to show you after the kids are in bed. No excuses."

Busted. He'd leapt at Connor's sledding suggestion when Evie had pulled out her laptop, her bridezilla frown firmly in place. He loved her, manic worries and all, but in the last month, he'd seriously regretted not eloping.

"Get on the toboggan, sunshine." He narrowed his eyes as he growled, but she just tipped her face up for another kiss.

He gave it to her. He always would.

Connor and Max swarmed around them, Ava giggling at her half-brothers. "Gentle," Evie reminded everyone. "Which sled can Ava use?"

They stayed outside until the light faded and the

bright stars came out. Stars he'd never seen in the city, it felt like. Blinking diamonds in the sky that reminded him of his woman.

Inside, they warmed up with a lentil stew that wasn't half bad, and store-bought brownies which were awesome. Evie took Ava off to bed while Liam and the boys devoured dessert. She reappeared with the dreaded laptop as they finished, rolling her eyes at Liam's obviously pained expression.

"I think the schedule needs to change again. And the centrepieces..."

"Just do whatever you want, sunshine. Seriously, it'll be great."

Her face crumpled in a genuine *I'm out of my league here* sadness that hit him like a punch in the gut.

"Okay. I promised Max I'd help him with his math homework, but then you've got me for the rest of the night."

Her relieved smile reached all the way to her eyes. "For the rest of my life. That's what's making all of this worthwhile."

Liam tugged her close and kissed her softly, and chastely, but not PG-13 enough for the boys.

"Oh, brother," Connor and Max said at the same time, their favourite catch phrase of the moment, applying it to all overt displays of affection.

Evie winked and left them to their homework.

Liam took a deep breath. Three weeks until the

honeymoon. He was going to make every second of those three days at the cottage in Pine Harbour count, because right now they were focusing on entirely the wrong things. *Centerpieces. Who the fuck cares?*

EVIE WOKE up in the middle of the night, worrying about centrepieces and impressing Liam's mother and a myriad of possible disasters that could ruin the biggest party she'd ever planned. They'd spent an hour going over everything before Ava woke up at eleven, crying about something they couldn't figure out, and Evie had brought her to bed. That was the last thing she remembered, because as was the case all too often lately, she'd fallen asleep as soon as her head hit the pillow.

With a heavy sigh, she rolled over, yelling at herself in her head to go back to sleep, and in protest of her impending full-consciousness, she refused to open her eyes. Sleepless nights were the worst. As she turned to the centre of the bed, instead of finding a snuggled-in toddler as she expected, her hand slid across warm man flesh.

"I moved Ava back to her room," Liam muttered, stirring under her touch. "Can't you sleep?"

Instead of answering, she circled her fingertips through the narrow line of silky hair leading south from his belly button. "Yeah. You awake?"

"I am now." His voice was rough with sleep, but also thick with arousal, and as she hit the waistband of his boxer briefs, she found something else thick. Liam approved. "Slide your hand in there."

She did. She always would.

His breathing quickly changed as she jerked him slowly. He swelled against her palm, hot velvety skin stretching into her touch, and when she pressed her breasts against his back, he groaned and reached back, sliding his hand blindly over her hip to cup her ass and hold her tight against him.

They jockeyed their arms for position before Liam flipped over and pinned her to the bed. Sliding his bare legs between her flannel covered ones, he kissed her roughly as he shoved up her tank top, ratcheting the heat of the moment up a thousand degrees.

Yes. She arched into his touch as he cupped her breasts, teasing her nipples into tight peaks before sucking her flesh hard into his mouth. He didn't linger there, just enough to get her panting, before he moved lower, stripping her out of her pj pants. They'd learned to take these stolen moments and make the most of them.

And Liam knew better than most men how to make the most of a wet, willing woman. He kissed his way up one thigh, groaning when he found her soaked for him. "You're so ready," he whispered.

"Then get up here and fuck me already," she said, her words strained and hungry.

"*I'm* not ready. It's been too long…" He trailed off as he stroked her folds open, circling her clit as he readied her for his mouth.

It had been almost a week. Between kids and wedding and work, they'd both been swamped. "Just think about our honeymoon. Three nights of sleeping naked together…"

"You think I'm going to let you sleep?" He laughed, his breath hot against her sex. "We can sleep here. That cottage is going to be our sex palace."

Now it was her turn to groan as he stopped talking and started licking. And sucking. And generally drove her out of her mind in less time than it would take a Formula 1 driver to hit top speed. She rocked her hips against his face, whining his name as he pushed her hard to the edge of the orgasmic cliff, and as soon as she flew over it, arms wide and mind blown, he was on top of her again, sliding deep.

It was the best feeling in the world, Liam making love to her like this, urgently but not hurried. Never hurried. One thing that she knew as truth—Liam always wanted more of her.

His mouth on her neck, his hands on her breasts and her bottom, he drove into her with heavy thrusts. Each slide dragged his erection over a million nerve endings and she shuddered beneath him, breathing his name. It felt even better than usual, which was saying something.

"You close? I need to pull out." He ground the words against her skin, his voice an abstract flutter, separate from the steady strokes his hips delivered not so slowly now.

Shit. No condom was a mood...changer. But not a killer. No, from the flood of moisture and the way her body arched to hold him deep inside her, the realization that Liam was bare inside her was a turn on. Damnit.

"Babe, you wanted to wait..."

"And you didn't," she crooned. "It's just a few more weeks."

It was too dark to see his face, not really, but in the faint light she imagined his eyes glinting down at her as he held himself over her for a second, then they were moving together in such synchronicity it took her breath away.

They both wanted this moment—it was why Evie had pushed to wait until after the wedding. Ava had been conceived by accident while Evie was in the city for a weekend escape from her reality as a single mom. That Liam had found her, and waited for her to come to her senses and fall in love with him, was a crazy miracle. That he loved her and their children and wanted more... it was the best thing she'd ever have in her entire life. And she wanted their next child to be conceived with intent.

The way Liam was holding on to her, and moving inside her...his intent was clear.

"You sure?" he asked, and her heart swelled so big she couldn't speak. Instead, she nodded, bringing his face to hers so he could feel the affirmation as she kissed him. With a bone-deep growl, he surged, stretching her wide, filling her up. She tangled her legs around his, writhing against him as he stoked her fire from the inside and she sought her own release on the outside, rocking against him at just the right place to see sparks and hear thunder as another orgasm hurtled her way.

He groaned her name against her lips as he tangled his fingers into her hair. She could imagine what they'd look like if there were any light in the room, his dark head pressed against her blonde hair, his lean, muscled body working hard to bring them both to climax. His ass would look so fine, clenching with each thrust. His legs, dusted with dark hair...

"Ahhhh!" Evie half-laughed, half-gasped as Liam came inside her, triggering her own orgasm. She squeezed her thighs around him, holding him deep inside her.

"Like that," he whispered as their hearts hammered hard against each other. He dragged air into his lungs. "Like that a lot."

Happiness skittered across her skin as she also sucked in a breath, still coming down from the awesome high. Yes. She liked it a lot, too.

2

———

NORMALLY the sight of her fiancé in a toolbelt and a hard hat would be enough to make Evie strip off her clothes and suggest a quickie, because Liam hard at work? There'd never be anything sexier.

But her thoughts were anything but romantic when she stopped by the inn four days before their wedding. She'd come to do her obsessive daily check of the final touches, and drop off the place cards and programs, fresh from the printer. The last thing she expected to find was the renovated mansion freezing cold and completely dark.

Standing in the brand new lobby, out of the wintery wind, Liam was talking to two other men in hard hats, and none of them looked happy.

Evie made an interrupting noise, politely at first,

then gave up pretending to care about decorum. "Why the hell is it dark in here?"

"Oh, hey." Liam flashed her a grin.

"Oh, hey? Liam!"

"We're fixing it." He winked and returned to his conversation, quietly talking about gas lines and generators.

Evie bit her lip. She was overly hormonal because she'd just finished her period. And she'd been disappointed that, having given Liam the green light, she hadn't gotten pregnant right away. It was silly. She knew in her heart it could take many cycles, but Ava had been...

She sighed. That was not where her head needed to be. Her emotions were strung tight with the warring anticipation and anxiety over the wedding. She didn't need to heap baby desire on top of that stew.

Liam quickly finished his conversation and waved to the contractors as they left. Which didn't fill Evie with hope. "Where are they going?"

"We've had to stop the final detail work until the electrician reconnects the power supply."

"What happened?" Tears threatened, and she steeled herself against them.

"A heavy tree branch fell on the main power line and ripped it from the building." Liam shook his head as she opened her mouth to launch into a million more questions. "It's going to be okay."

"You promise?"

He closed the gap between them, flashing his lopsided sexy smirk that always worked on her. "I promise we'll get married on Saturday."

"Here."

"Somewhere." He leaned in for a kiss but she dodged her head to the side, just letting his lips graze her cheek. The second he kissed her, she'd be fine with whatever, and *whatever* was definitely not fine. Not with their guest list.

"Your mother!" *And all her fancy friends.*

"Our generators are being installed tomorrow. So even if the electrician has problems restoring power today—and I don't think he will—we're probably going to be fine."

"She's going to call me a hick. A hick and a hack, for trying to hold this wedding in this *sleepy backwater*." She knew her voice was shaking. She couldn't help it. Liam's mother had pushed for them to have a society wedding in Toronto, and Evie had insisted Wardham could be fancy enough.

Tears threatened as she realized that claim had been balanced on a wish and a prayer, totally contingent on Liam getting the inn ready ahead of schedule. And now the worst had happened—their tightly packed schedule had been derailed by a mishap.

"Sunshine, you can't worry about..." He trailed off when her eyes flared wide—this wasn't the first time they'd had this fight. At least he had the good sense to cut himself off. "Okay, you *can* worry about it, if you want to, but you know it's illogical, right?"

"Shut up."

"Do you kiss our children with that mouth?" Another grin.

"Don't distract me with charm."

"But it works every time, right?" This time his kiss landed true, and she let him in because he was her rock. If he didn't care about a major hiccup a few days before their wedding, neither would she. On the outside. He pressed a little deeper, as if he could chase away her fears from the inside out, his tongue teasing hers even as his lips curled into another smile. "Stop thinking about it. Do you have a pretty dress?"

"Yes."

"And I've got this super sexy tool belt. And a marriage license. The kids are excited." That was true. Ava had been tossing fake flower petals around their house for weeks and Connor and Max were proud to be a part of the ceremony too—they had a poem to read, and they were giving the rings to Liam. She knew he was right, but her stomach still felt like it was going to flip inside out any second. "The important stuff is sorted. That's all that matters, right?"

"No, impressing your mother is all that matters." She peeked up at him through narrowed eyelids, smiling hopefully. "No?"

"Not even a little bit."

"She scares me."

"That's silly. My father's the truly terrifying one." Liam slid his hand around the base of her neck, tucking his fingers under the braid poking out the bottom of her toque. "Four more days, then a big party. Then three nights...all alone. Think about that part."

"Mmmm." She lifted her mouth to his, letting his kiss get under her skin this time. "No kids."

"No family."

"No clothes."

"God, Evie..." He tightened his grip on her nape and sucked her lower lip between his before pulling away, hungry regret bright in his eyes. "I've gotta get back to work."

"Okay. I love you." She said, a whisper against his mouth because he was already going back in for another kiss.

"It's going to be okay. Our wedding is going to be perfect, sunshine."

———

THEIR WEDDING WAS GOING to be a disaster.

Not the getting married part—Liam couldn't wait to put a ring on Evie's finger, knock her up again, and get back to their crazy life of spaghetti dinners, Lego battles, and making sure they had pants on before falling asleep because they never woke up alone.

He wouldn't have it any other way.

But first they had to have the biggest wedding Wardham had ever seen, with a ridiculous delegation of Toronto's rich and famous arriving in the next forty-eight hours, and there wouldn't be anywhere for those guests to stay.

Liam didn't tell Evie about the extra drama—when the power loss happened, the sump pump stopped working and the basement flooded. No good would come of her knowing that.

Even if they got the power fixed today, the house-keeping staff—still just a skeleton crew at this point—was a solid day behind schedule. No matter which way he turned the puzzle in his mind, Liam couldn't see a path that didn't end with his Aunt Edith saying some-thing about standards being lower in *the country*, and Evie turning into a raging mama bear. Which he wouldn't really mind—her fierceness was one of the things he most loved about her. It had taken months to crack her shell after their one-night stand.

His beautiful woman. So totally open to adventure... as long as her children were protected. And in this scenario, their quiet little town of Wardham would be the child, all innocent and special.

It didn't help that his mother had refused to stay the night on their only visit from the city, a few weeks after

Ava was born, because of the lack of acceptable facilities.

Liam had no interest in pushing her. His uncle Ted—who lived across the road from Claire Calhoun, Evie's mother—had no love lost for his sister-in-law. Liam's aunt had passed ten years earlier, and his mother hadn't spent long in town for the funeral, either.

But Evie wanted their daughter to have contact with everyone, so they'd travelled to Toronto twice for awkward family visits. More trips than Liam had wanted, but every time his parents asked, Evie said yes.

And then worried about matching outfits for the boys and whether or not Liam needed a haircut.

Evie didn't worry very well. She wasn't bred to worry like his family was. A farm girl, his fiancée was built of sterner stuff—with a healthy dose of unbridled optimism, to boot. But his mother—and not the real woman, but the myth of Amelia McIntosh, and all the society page references that implied—got under Evie's skin in the worst way.

And she kept going back for more. It started with an email.

"I should ask your mother about the seating arrangements," Evie had said a few weeks before Christmas. They were on the couch, exchanging foot rubs and talking about the wedding plans, back when the wedding still danced in the nearish distance as a fun future event.

Liam had winced, and that started a back and forth that got a bit testy, so then he'd distracted her by dragging her to bed and getting naked.

That only worked for a few hours.

"She'll appreciate the inclusion," Evie murmured over breakfast while scrubbing peanut butter off Max's face.

Liam winced and poured his fiancée a cup of coffee before diving in. "She'll say the wrong thing and hurt your feelings."

Round and round they went, Evie winning, only to find out that Liam had been right.

They repeated the same pattern over the rehearsal dinner plans and the music for the mother-son dance.

Now they were four days out, Evie was convinced their wedding was a hick-splosion of tackiness, and their guests didn't have anywhere to sleep.

His phone rang, and Liam breathed a sigh of relief at his "best man's" number on the screen. "Jessica Doran, you better be calling to tell me you're showing up early tomorrow."

A watery laugh told him more trouble was about to land in his lap. "How about I'm coming late and alone? And I might cry my way through your wedding—to the most beautiful woman in the world, who you probably don't deserve—and then I'll leave early because of the aforementioned aloneness?"

"What the hell happened?" Liam had never liked

Jess's husband, Brent. For most of the time he'd known his friend, Brent had been her on-again, off-again boyfriend. Then they'd taken a weekend trip to Vegas four months ago and come back as husband and wife. "Bring him. I'll kill him."

"Can't bring him, he's moved out."

"Seriously? Speaking of beautiful women and the men that don't deserve them—"

"Leave it, please, Liam. I didn't call you to hear a list of all the things you hate about Brent."

"It's a long list." It really wasn't. Brent actually seemed like a decent enough guy, but there'd always been something about him that rubbed Liam the wrong way—how he didn't give Jessica his all, probably. Liam never had any time for selfishness, especially not when it came to a friend's heart.

"I'm still coming."

"Good. Bring alcohol."

"Oh shit, what's happened?"

Liam filled her in on the problems at the inn, and his general anxiety about his parents spending an entire weekend in Wardham—or not spending the whole weekend. He was damned if they did, and damned if they didn't.

"Okay, so we'll all stay somewhere else."

"There isn't anywhere else. There are a few bed and breakfasts in Kingsville, and hotels in Windsor. That's it. Hardly the winter weekend in the country that Evie's planned out so carefully. If they stay somewhere else, they'll just come for the wedding and none of the other stuff will happen."

"She's still intent on proving to your mother that Wardham is like Sleepy Hollow, or Bar Harbor, or something out of a Martha Stewart magazine?" Jess sighed. "I can't blame her. It's really the loveliest little town, but I can't see your parents ever getting that."

"Frankly, I don't care if they do."

"Hmmm."

"What, hmmm?"

"Nothing. I'll talk to Evie about it."

"No. Don't do that. Don't cut me out of your psychic girl connection. It's not real. It's not science."

"Liam!" He was really done with women shrieking his name at him like that today. "Trust me. I'm a woman, I know what she's feeling right now."

He snorted, but then immediately felt guilty when Jess sniffled again. "Fine, tell me where I've gone wrong."

"She just wants to know she's loved unconditionally and accepted for who she is. Except in this case, she's conflated her own identity with that of her town, and you with your entire extended family and former society life."

Shit. "I hate it when you're right."

3

———

FIVE hours later, Liam looked around his soon-to-be mother-in-law's kitchen at the hastily formed Wedding Rescue committee. "Everyone know what they've got to do? We're going to make this town shine this weekend, right?"

Evan West nodded and unfolded himself from one of the kitchen chairs. If anyone in Wardham could make Liam feel unsophisticated, it was the older West brother—international businessman, mysterious sex symbol, all around good guy. But instead of feeling competitive—which he'd expected, since Evan had been Evie's first serious boyfriend—the other man had welcomed him to town and contracted him when the winery had need of Liam's project management skill set. An interesting friendship had formed.

Liam still didn't get the guy, but he liked him a lot. More importantly, he trusted him.

He trusted Chase Miller and Ian Nixon, too, both good guys, but also because they'd been sent as delegates by Evie's best friends.

On the other hand, this was a *wedding* emergency, and they were all guys.

The women were busy. One of them, Karen Miller—Evie's best friend, and Chase's older sister—was in labour, and the others were taking care of her. Tea and back rubs, Liam assumed. Whatever kept Evie distracted was good, and a new baby was always worthy of celebration. And maybe what this wedding needed was some out-of-the-box, testosterone-fuelled creativity.

"You boys can keep a secret, right?" Liam ruffled Max's hair and winked at Connor. His step-sons, who'd accepted him in their lives before their mother had, bless her prickly heart, were all in favour of the plan.

"Good secrets." Max whispered, taking his solemn task *very* seriously.

"That's right. And making your mom happy is a very good thing."

"Maybe another wedding present could be teaching Ava how to use a sippy cup. That really seems to annoy Mom," Connor deadpanned, before cracking his face into a smile.

"I know it does," Liam said, scooping up his toddling daughter, who kept bumping into his legs as she searched for a rice cracker. He'd brought all three kids with him because he'd sent Evie out the door the second she got the phone call from her friend. And *then* he'd gotten the brain wave that would fix the wedding fiasco.

Bed and breakfasts. Of the highest quality. So he'd made some calls, and summoned everyone to the farm, where Evie wouldn't find them.

The beds would be sourced by Ian Nixon, born and raised in Wardham.

Evie's mother, Claire, had graciously offered to host Liam's parents herself. The Calhoun farm was picturesque. Perfect.

The quality would be overseen by Evan, who'd already taken on the task of Master of Ceremonies for the wedding reception. He'd have his winery staff put together welcome baskets for each out-of-town guest, and personally deliver them to each residence hosting Liam's family and friends.

"What about transportation?" Evan asked as he walked closer. He wiggled his index finger at Ava, who buried her face in Liam's shoulder and squealed. He did it again, and this time, Ava reached out and grabbed on.

Liam saw an opportunity and grabbed it. "Here, you take her for a second, I need to make some notes."

"Whoa..." Evan laughed nervously as Liam's little angel launched herself at her honorary uncle. "Aren't you pretty. And...damp."

Liam glanced up from his phone. "Probably water."

"Might be a leaky poop," Max offered helpfully, as only a seven year old could.

Evan jerked straight up, looking only slightly panicked, and Liam arched a brow in challenge. *Take it like a man.* And Evan did. "Is there a bag or something? Do you want me to…"

Liam laughed. "Nah. You'd know if she had a dirty diaper. I'm sure she was just dumping her sippy cup on the floor."

"Here, I'll go find her some new pants." Claire swooped in, taking Ava despite Evan's protests that he was fine. "And maybe some craft stuff for you two?" She pointed at Max and Connor.

Liam shook his head. "Let them stay. They're important committee members."

Max grinned proudly, and Liam's heart squeezed tight. He refocused on the list on his phone, pretending he wasn't a giant sap for those kids. "Okay, we'll need a shuttle bus. Or limos? Ideas?"

"School buses!" Max and Connor said at the same time, dissolving into giggles and claims of jinx and owing each other sodas.

Liam winced.

"No…" Chase said slowly, looking at Evan first, who nodded, then Ian, who shrugged. "That could work. Play up the small town thing, instead of ignoring it. We don't have stretch Hummers here, and that's okay. We've got school buses, and they've got heaters, and—"

"Hot chocolate," Ian interjected.

Evan grinned. "And hot apple cider and tartan blankets. But will Evie hate it?"

Liam liked that he alone knew the answer to that. These might be her childhood friends, and Evan might have been her first lover, but Liam was going to be her husband for the rest of their lives. "She's not going to get it at first. And there'll be some yelling and scowling. But it's perfect."

"I know the general manager at Henkel's Bussing. I'll give him a call." Ian stood and pulled out his phone.

"What else can I do?" Chase asked.

Liam nodded. "I think I need a favour from your woman."

———

"I CAN'T DO THIS."

Evie suppressed a smile and leaned on the other side of the exercise ball Karen was using for support. "You're so strong, lady. You've got this."

"I want all the drugs. Let's go to the hospital—arrrghh!" Her friend's face contorted and turned white as another contraction ramped up quickly. Beside her, the midwives were setting out everything they needed to safely deliver the baby who was about to make his arrival into the world. They were in Karen and Paul's bedroom on the second floor of their craftsman style-bungalow, just a few blocks from Evie's house. Down-stairs, Carrie Nixon was watching a movie with Megan, Paul's daughter from his first marriage. It was the middle of the night, but the eleven year old couldn't sleep. She was too excited to meet her little brother.

Evie understood the feeling completely. Births were a wonderful thing. But unlike Megan, she didn't want to wait downstairs until the messy stuff was done. This was the first labour she'd attended, other than her own three, and she was pumped.

Way more so than the hard-working mama, it seemed. Karen sagged forward as the last pulses of the contraction faded from her body. "That one was hard," she whispered, a sob wracking her voice. Evie under-stood the feeling, and she'd done this before. Karen was a first-time mom, and the only way to truly understand the craziness of birth was to go through it.

"This is good," the midwife murmured in her ear. "Let it out. Let the tears come."

"Where's Paul?" Karen twisted her head, looking blindly for her husband.

"Right here. I'm right here." He'd been kneeling behind her quietly, just rubbing her back, for the last half hour as she went through the painful contractions and final dilation of transition.

"Too hard, baby," she whimpered, and in chorus, everyone else in the room reminded her to deepen her vocalizations. To which Karen responded with a much heartier, "Fuck you all."

Laughter rocked Evie's core. "That's the spirit."

"No, seriously." Karen groaned, giving up her protest as she curled over her belly again. Evie watched, fascinated, as the midwives quietly discussed the little things they were noticing about Karen's body and actions.

"Okay, Karen, we think you might be ready to start pushing. Do you want us to check to make sure you're fully dilated? Or do you feel baby bearing down?"

"I don't know." She closed her eyes and let out a long sigh. "Can I take a nap?"

They waited out two more contractions, letting Karen catch a bit of rest between them, but on the third one, she started pushing, and before Evie knew it, she was being bumped to the side. The midwives helped Karen into a squat, leaning back against Paul, and rearranged the disposable sterile pads underneath her.

It was like time stood still, watching her friend go through the last few pushes, working so hard to bring her baby into the world. And when he arrived, it was with a lusty yell that brought tears to Evie's eyes.

She wasn't the only one. She snuck a look at Paul, his face buried in Karen's shoulder as he helped her hold their newborn to her chest. "I'm going to check on Megan," she whispered, leaving the parents to a moment of privacy.

Downstairs, she found the pre-teen asleep on the couch, so she gave Carrie the good news.

Before long, one of the midwives quietly came down and told them Karen and Paul were asking for Megan. They woke her, and she scampered upstairs to meet her baby brother.

"You should go home," Carrie said quietly. "You've got a lot to do in the next three days."

"So do you." Evie yawned, then laughed. "Great reason to miss sleep, though. That was awesome."

Carrie grinned. "You're such a birth junkie."

"Guilty."

"Go home. I have to be at the bakery in an hour anyway to get the muffins going, and I can go home as soon as my part-timers arrive and open the shop."

"You sure?"

"Absolutely. A bride needs her beauty rest. I'm going to go up and see the baby, then head to work. I have a wedding cake to get started on."

"I don't think I can handle anything else going wrong. If you drop it, just patch it up and never tell me, okay?"

"Wouldn't be the first time." Her laughter died as Evie's mouth dropped open. "I mean…"

"It's okay," Evie said weakly. "I'm starting to think I'm just not cut out for this wedding business."

It was a short drive home from Karen's house, through the frosty, quiet streets of Wardham. Liam had parked his SUV as far over to the right as he could, so she could pull past him on the one and a half wide driveway. The little things that man did for her...she seriously couldn't count them all.

Inside, she checked on her kids, all fast asleep in their beds. Only one of them, Ava, was wearing pyjamas, but the boys in their boxers and t-shirts and scrubbed faces were pretty cute. Just like their step-dad, who she found equally sleepy in her own bed. But as always, he roused as she slid in next to him.

"Any baby news?"

"They named him William," she whispered. "He's beautiful."

"I bet." Liam grinned, a sleepy, loopy smile that made her stomach do flip flops. "Did you suggest Liam as a nickname?"

She laughed and curled into his side. "They seem content with Will for now."

"That's good, too."

"Mmm." She closed her eyes as he ran his fingers through her hair. "I have to be up in two hours to make lunches. I should have done it before I came to bed."

"I'll do it."

"Yeah?"

"Shut up with that surprise, sunshine. Of course I'll do it."

"You're a great dad."

He didn't say anything to that, just hugged her close.

She thought he'd fallen asleep again, but after a minute he asked about Karen, and Paul, and she told him a little about the birth. She fell asleep with him stroking her hair, murmuring softly in her ear about what he remembered from Ava's birth.

BY noon the next day, Evie was done with work at her Pilates studio on the quiet main drag of Wardham—growing less quiet by the month, as more and more businesses moved into the increasingly popular day-tourism town. But nobody was beach-bound in February, so her only clients were her regulars, no drop-ins, and they'd all understand. Even though she wasn't officially done—there were two more classes that afternoon, and a small stack of bills to pay, plus she needed to place an order for water bottles and exercise mats—her heart and head just weren't in it. She was in the midst of making a "Closed Until After The Wedding" sign, complete with a free class coupon to make up for anyone's inconvenience, when Liam's best friend walked in.

There weren't many people Evie liked as much as

Jessica Doran. She was one of those strong, pulled-together women that still managed to be humble, self-effacing, and genuinely nice. Plus she always brought red wine when she visited.

Today, though, she didn't look great. Of course, she *looked* great. Tall, curvy, with shiny brown hair in sculpted waves to just below her shoulder and rocking a *leggings and sweater with tall boots* look, Jess was pretty as ever. But her gaze was *broken*.

"What's wrong?" Evie flew around the counter and gave her friend a hug.

"Didn't Liam tell you? I talked to him yesterday."

Evie shook her head. "Sorry, no. We had some excitement last night—a friend had a baby, and I was out until early morning. What's going on?"

"I told Liam I wouldn't come down until tomorrow, but I figured he could use my help, and I'm just happy to get out of the house..." The corners of her mouth dropped in the saddest frown ever. "Brent's left me."

"Oh my god. Honey, I'm so sorry." Evie shook her head. "I want to hear everything, if you're able, or nothing if you're not. Give me three minutes to close up here and we can head back to my place."

"No, I don't want to derail the wedding work. Surely you've got a to-do list I can start chipping away at? When does your sister get into town?"

"In a few hours." Evie grinned. One thing she was unreservedly looking forward to—a weekend of girly fun with Laney. "We're having a girls' night tonight. Heavy on the red wine, light on the squealing."

"Yeah? I'm in." Jess narrowed her eyes. "You're telling the truth?"

"About the red wine, yes. Could go either way on the squealing. Depends on what scandalous secrets are revealed."

"Deal."

———

THAT NIGHT, Liam organized pizza for dinner, then he and Kyle took charge of the kids' bedtime. It was a fun co-ed hangout for a bit as Jess got to know Evie's sister and brother-in-law, but once the kids were asleep, the men made themselves scarce, heading to Wardham's only pub, Danny's, for a drink. They made mumbling sounds about meeting Evan and Chase there.

"It might just be the three of us tonight," Eve said apologetically to her sister as the three women settled on the couches in Evie's living room. "Mari and Stella are working tonight, Karen just had a baby, and Carrie is catching up on sleep after staying up all night in antici- pation for that baby."

"How is Karen doing?"

"Good. Jess dropped me by there this afternoon for a quick visit while she ran decorations to the church. Little Will is so cute. It's hard to remember Ava ever being that small. I look forward to those precious first few days and weeks again. Next time I'll try to enjoy them more."

"Next time? Are you thinking of another one already?" Laney stared at her incredulously and took a big gulp of red wine. "No offence."

"Ha. None taken. You're missing out. Babies are awesome."

"But four of them?" Her sister shook her head. "I'm just being rude now, I know. I'll shut up."

From the look on Jess's face, she shared the same surprise, but was doing a better job of keeping it to herself. Evie just shrugged. "What can I say? Liam makes me want to procreate. The man makes good babies."

Jess laughed. "You have a fair hand in that, too. And Ava is adorable. But your boys are gorgeous, too. And funny. And well-behaved." She frowned into her wine glass for a minute, but instead of sharing more, she changed the subject. "Tell me about the studio. How's it going?"

A business analyst for a major bank, Jess never tired of hearing about the ins and outs of small business ownership. And Laney was a big supporter, too, being the proud sister. So, Evie indulged in a little bragging about expanding her class offerings, and hiring Stella and making that investment pay off.

"Next thing you know, there will be a chain of

Wardham Pilates studios." Laney giggled. "Might need to change the name. No one will know what it means."

"Hey, speaking of name changes," Evie said. "Guess what Carrie told me last night? Dale wants to formally petition the town council to change the name of the beach."

Laney groaned, and Jess looked back and forth between them in confusion. "Who's Dale? And what's the name of the beach?"

Evie rolled her eyes. "Dale is my ex-husband. He's going to run for town council in the next election, which is...fine. He's not a bad guy, just a bit hot-headed. And stubborn."

Laney snorted. "It's no wonder you guys didn't work out."

"Yeah, no kidding. But we got two gorgeous kids out of it. And now I have Liam." She grinned.

"God, you two are so ridiculously in love, it's...ridiculous." Jess sighed. "Continue. Beach story."

"So our beach...well it doesn't really have a name. It's just the Wardham Municipal Beach. Because...we're not fancy. End of story."

"Oh." Jess scrunched her face up in thought.

"Oh?"

"Well, what does he suggest instead?" Jess shrugged. "Re-naming to be more marketable isn't the worst idea."

"He has no idea. His genius plan is to pay a marketing firm to 're-brand' the town."

"That's ridiculous. You don't need to pay money for it. Run a contest, pick the best idea." Jess lifted the bottle. "More?"

Evie slowly looked at Laney, then back at Jess. "That's a great idea."

Jess shrugged. "I do some volunteer marketing for a couple of charities in London. I'd love to help. It's actually what my focus was in biz school, but I couldn't find a job for it in London, so now I'm in banking."

"Well, if you ever want to move here and run for town council, I'll help you kick my ex's ass. Or just come here and be smart. You should talk to Evan West about business stuff at the wedding. He's our emcee, you'll meet him Friday night at the rehearsal dinner."

"Speaking of which," Laney smoothly interrupted. "What's on the agenda tomorrow?"

"We have to go out to the winery and check on the progress at the inn. Liam's been dodging my questions about it, so I'm worried they're cutting corners to get it ready. That's not acceptable. I need to pick up my dress from the shop in Exeter, and if we have time, I'd like to go to Windsor and get something for Liam's mother. What impresses incredibly wealthy women who have everything?"

"Nothing," Laney and Jess said at the same time.

Evie frowned. That sounded like the right answer—and they would know better—but it wasn't what she wanted to hear.

"Why do you want to get her something? Won't Liam give her flowers or something? A corsage?"

"I went with mini bouquets for the mothers, I thought that was classier," Evie said, chewing on her lip.

Laney nodded. "I like that."

"But really," Jess said, shaking her head. "That's totally enough. It's *your* wedding."

"I just want her to be impressed." Evie wrinkled her nose. "I know, it's silly. Liam keeps telling me it doesn't matter."

Laney stood up. "He's right. I'm going to grab some hummus and tortilla chips."

"Oooh, good idea! There's some salsa in the fridge, too," Evie said, watching her sister leave the room. When she turned back, Jess had that scrunched-up, thinking face on again. "What?"

"Can I be honest?"

"Of course. We've had wine, anything goes."

"Maybe you don't believe Liam because he's not addressing your real concern."

"What do you mean?"

"Are you anxious about impressing Liam's family for you, or for him?"

"Liam doesn't care." At least not on the surface.

"I know he says he doesn't." Jess leaned in and gentled her voice. "But he's not that emotionally available in any other part of his life, is he?"

No. Liam struggled with voicing his feelings sometimes, but he never, ever had any difficulty showing them or putting her and the kids first.

"Do you think...Shit." Evie swallowed hard. "Shit shit shit. I'm a terrible wife. And I'm not even a wife yet. Of course he cares, and instead of seeing that, I've been making it worse."

"I didn't say that." Jess leaned forward and pressed her hand to Evie's knee. "Stop spinning."

"It's three days before my wedding, I don't think that's possible."

"Listen to me for a second. You can't fix whatever rift there is between Liam and his parents."

Evie stared at her friend for a second. "What? Of course I can, I've just been going about it the wrong way."

"The problem isn't you, or your town, or your family not being impressive enough."

Evie frowned. "Where did you get that from?"

"Liam said a few things, little things, yesterday on the phone, and I filled in the gaps."

"Oh."

"Liam's parents...I don't know them that well, but Liam and I studied closely together for two years in the city where they live, and I think he saw them a grand total of four times in that period. They weren't close when he was on the MBA track, and that was pretty impressive."

Evie chewed on her lip some more.

"Wow, the mood in here got heavy," Laney quipped as she returned with a tray of munchies.

"Ugh." Evie dug in to the salsa. "I've been banging my head against a brick wall for no reason, that's all."

"The mother problem?"

"Yep. So what do I do?"

Jess shrugged. "Obviously I'm no expert, because I foolishly got married on a whim in Vegas—"

"Hey, that's not foolish," Laney interrupted. She'd eloped the previous year as well, surprising Kyle in spectacular style while he was in Vegas for work.

Jess scowled darkly. "Easy for you to say, I presume your husband still loves you?"

"Sorry." Laney winced and lifted the wine bottle. "More, yes?"

They all laughed and held out their glasses. *Hell, yes.*

Jess took a big gulp, then pointed at Evie. "You should have the wedding you want, and let it be the happiest day of your life, no matter what."

Laney nodded. "Let Liam worry about his parents."

"But what if they never—"

Jess held up her hand. "Then they never. And that's okay. Now... I was promised scandalous secrets. Spill."

———

BY THE TIME Liam and Kyle got home from the pub, two of the three women were lolling back in their seats, half-asleep and silly-happy on quite a lot of wine. Laney gave Liam a high-five on her way out the door, after letting him know none of the kids had woken up and she'd be back first thing to do all things wedding.

He made up the couch for Jess and carefully steered Evie to the bathroom to brush her teeth, then tucked her in.

The plan had been to tell her about the inn and new accommodations plan tonight—Evan had met them at the pub, and Mari had been behind bar, so Chase was on his stool, as usual, playing guard dog over his fiancée, so they had another secret committee meeting.

The bad news was, the electrician had to get into the exterior wall, and while there was a temporary patch, he'd be back the next day to do more work. The good news was, none of them thought it was that big a deal, and Evan had roped Beth Stewart, his director of operations and a woman who knew and liked Evie, to take care of the alternate arrangements.

It sounded so reasonable.

He couldn't tell her over breakfast. There would be yelling, and someone had to think of the children. He glanced at the closed bedroom door. On the other side was his good friend Jess. Maybe *she* could tell Evie.

No, he needed to man up. He'd go to work for the morning and connect with her at lunch time. Maybe tell her in a public space...

He gave his head a shake and climbed into bed.

Sliding his hand over Evie's hip, he curled himself around her back. "I can't wait until this wedding nonsense is behind us," he whispered.

"Snot nonsense," she mumbled. "Big deal. Love."

"Yep. That's what makes it worthwhile, sunshine. I promise it's going to be wonderful."

"Mmmm..." Her mumble turned into a soft snore before she could finish her incomprehensible thought, and he kissed her hair and closed his eyes.

———

IT TURNED out that Beth Stewart, the operations manager at the winery, knew a lot of people with really lovely homes in Wardham. The next day, she texted him that all the rooms were sorted out, and by early afternoon, Liam was standing with her and Evan West on the sidewalk outside the six bedroom Wilkins' home. The stately, yellow-brick mansion, half a block off the main drag, would hold most of his extended family, except his parents, who had been unexpectedly gracious about the change in plans when he called them that morning. His college friends and business colleagues would be staying at five other homes nearby—close enough that Beth could point at most of the homes, all in the original part of the village. Liam had never really noticed these four square blocks, near the town hall, but they were decidedly picturesque.

The suspiciously fresh looking pine boughs decorating the light standards on each corner might have something to do with the appeal. The boughs matched some of the wintery decorations gracing the front entrances of the nearby homes.

"I can't thank you guys enough for all of this work."

Evan shrugged. "We were going to provide them all accommodation at the inn. This is no different."

Beth nodded. "And I bet I can convince some of these people to be overflow accommodation in the future, which means we can take on larger conferences. Necessity is the mother of invention, right? We owe *you* for getting married here and having such a big wedding. It's been a good trial run for our guest services." She winced. "Which obviously needed some work."

"I promise, as a customer, I'm very happy right now. The welcome baskets you organized look perfect."

"I'll touch base with each host tomorrow morning, and report back as people arrive. Will they be transporting themselves to the rehearsal dinner?"

"Yes, the buses are just for the day of the wedding."

"How's Evie taking all the last minute change?"

"Well...."

"Liam!" Beth scolded, not quite in a shriek but close enough.

"I wanted to tell her once everything was sorted out. I'm going to find her this afternoon, take her to Bun to see the wedding cake, ply her with a soy latte and carefully outline how everything is totally fine."

"Mmm-hmmm. I think we all want tickets to that." Beth pursed her lips and Evan, who'd been silent through the whole exchange, covered his face in a poor attempt to disguise his amusement.

"She'll be fine. All of this is going to make the wedding memorable."

"Touching speeches and adorable pictures of children sitting under tables are memorable wedding moments." Beth crossed her arms. "A complete overhaul of the major details the week of...that's traumatic."

"But everything's going to be fine. Better, even."

"Don't say that."

"Why not?"

"You're not usually this dense."

No, he wasn't. But he'd never gotten married before. It was a big thing they were doing, that would change almost nothing about their lives, but forever alter their souls. He wasn't stupid. He knew Evie had thought about this more than he had. Cared more. Worried more.

But he was taking care of things. It was all going to be okay.

Beth was still staring at him, expecting...what, he couldn't say, when his phone rang.

He lifted it to his ear. "Hello again, Mother."

"William. We were just discussing the new arrangements…"

He'd already started a slow, steady exhale before she'd finished her thought, and maybe because of that self-preservation technique, he actually missed what she said.

"Do you think that would be acceptable?"

"Pardon?"

"Would Claire be amenable to our early arrival?"

"Early arrival?" Okay, maybe the wedding was making him dense.

"Yes. As I said, we've discussed it and think it would be too chaotic to arrive tomorrow, before the rehearsal dinner. Your father has informed the office that he'll be away an extra day."

Oh. Shit. "Today?"

"We're leaving soon, darling. Perhaps you can find us a restaurant to take Evelyn and the children for dinner? Some place nice."

Liam stared dumbly at the phone in his hand for a minute after his mother ended the call. Finally Beth patted him on the shoulder, kissed him on the cheek, and said, "I assume we won't see you back at work this afternoon?"

No. He had a fiancée to find, surprise, placate and mollify…and a dinner reservation to make. "Wait! I need a favour!"

It was starting to become his catch phrase.

5

WHEN Liam texted her mid-afternoon with an **SOS, Come Home Quick** message, Evie assumed he was feeling frisky and wanted a belated nooner. She sent Jess and Laney to the florist shop to be bridezillas-by-proxy, and zipped to her house with a smile on her face.

It fell off when he told her his parents were en route, and they'd be staying at her mother's place, and it was all fine and dandy and her friends all had a plan. She just stared at him, dumbly, wondering if he was punking her, as he outlined the new ideas.

He didn't look like this was a prank. He leaned in, concern written all over his handsome, traitorous features. "Are you okay?"

She blinked a few times. "So you didn't want to have a quickie?"

"Is that on the table?"

She didn't bother to answer. She'd already flown to the boys' room, searching for something acceptable for them to wear. He followed her, half-laughing until she glowered at him so hard, it was a miracle he didn't spontaneously combust.

"I'll give you the world's longest back rub tonight."

She shrugged and stuffed two dark blue polo shirts into a bag, then pulled them out again and carefully rolled them to prevent wrinkles.

"What can I do?"

"Work some kind of magic and get the inn ready for tomorrow morning?"

"Babe, that ship has sailed."

"And you knew that two days ago when I came to see you."

She brushed past him, heading for the nursery.

"I didn't want you to worry."

"This is better than worry?"

"No."

The boys would wear khakis and polos. Ava could wear...she rifled through the closet. Ava had nothing for dinner with fancy-pants grandparents because she never saw them. "Why don't your parents have more of a relationship with our daughter?"

"I don't know. You can ask them tonight."

"I'm not starting a thing before the wedding!"

"Okay..." He stepped up behind her, wrapping his arms around her waist. "Hey. Stop for a second."

"You can't charm your way out of this one."

"I already have. Quaint, first-class bed and breakfasts? Come on, you're a little impressed."

"If I wanted a *quaint* wedding, I'd have planned one."

He kissed that spot under her ear, the one that made her melt, and he did it just right—scant pressure, more a promise than a true kiss, with a puff of hot breath and a greedy inhale at the end. He was good, she had to give him that. "And if you wanted a slick, urban wedding, you'd have moved our wedding to Windsor or Toronto. Everyone here would have been happy to travel for a weekend."

He wasn't wrong.

She closed her eyes. "What if it's all hokey?"

"Say what you will about Wardham. We might have drama, and everyone might get in everyone else's business, but we're never hokey."

She turned slowly in his arms. "We?" She grinned, amused at the surprise all over his face. "You think of yourself as one of us?"

A slow, cocky-as-hell smile crawled up his face. "Damn straight. Did that get me out of jail?"

"Mmm-hmm." She tugged his face down and kissed the tip of his nose.

"Do we have time for that nooner?"

They did not, but she gave him a long, lingering kiss,

and giggled as he complained good-naturedly about the resulting hard-on. It seemed like a fair punishment.

Three hours later, Evie stared around the farmhouse kitchen as Beth, Stella and a sous chef from the winery, whom she'd never met before, scurried around, transforming the house where she grew up into a fancy, television-esque version of the same thing. Shiny-clean, filled with flowers, and like there wasn't anything weird at all about having a uniformed waitress standing by, or a personal chef setting up a buffet in the corner.

"I'm going upstairs to get the kids dressed," she said faintly.

Her mother smiled at her, as if this were no big deal and kind of fun.

Surprises two days before your wedding were never fun.

Never.

"Thought you were okay with all of this," Liam whispered after following her up to the kids' bedroom. She'd lived with her mother for a year after her divorce, and when she bought her house, her mother kept the space pretty much as they had set it up for the boys. Now there was a crib in the corner, and it was primarily a playroom, although the kids had the occasional sleepover with Grandma.

Right now, it was a refuge from the elaborate show being prepared downstairs.

"Okay? Yes, of course. Confident? Hmm. Not so

much." She picked Ava up off the floor and slowly unsnapped her onesie. "Look at that. She's got mystery purple marks on her shirt."

"So?" He covered her shaking hands with his, and bumped his head gently into hers. Connor glanced over from where he was lying on one of the twin beds, playing with his iPod Touch. She offered him a weak smile. Liam lowered his voice for her ears only. "I love you, Evie. Nothing else matters, okay?"

She twisted her face away from the kids and into his shoulder. "I don't want anything else to go wrong," she whispered, closing her eyes.

"Nothing's gone wrong yet," he said, his voice a slow, steady stream of confidence. "Just changed. It's fun and exciting."

"I don't think I like excitement anymore."

He laughed, and then she joined him, because wrapped in her fiancé's warmth as he curved his body around hers, watching her kids be kids, and her baby protest being changed, her freakout seemed silly.

The butterflies didn't disappear, though, and as she pulled herself together and got the boys going on washing their faces and putting on their dinner clothes, she tried not to dwell on the fact that she still didn't know why she was so worried.

———

FROM THE SECOND FLOOR, Liam saw the dark Mercedes sedan that could only be his father's pull into the lane. He left Evie upstairs with the kids. He didn't announce his parents' arrival—she'd hear them soon enough, and better if he could gauge their mood first. Figure out what his expectations should be for the evening, and the weekend.

Apprehension pooled at the base of his neck, cold and heavy. This wasn't going to go *badly*. It never did. But with only two days before their wedding, he wanted it to go *well*, for Evie's sake.

He stepped out into the winter cold and watched from the porch as his father walked stiffly around the vehicle and opened the passenger door for Amelia McIntosh, secretly of Wardham.

If it bothered her, staying across the road from her brother's farm, she hadn't let on when Liam first told her Claire asked to host them for the weekend. He didn't know if she truly didn't care or if she'd locked down the part of her that might. That had always been his mother's great failing in his eyes—that she was fine with emotional vacancy.

He grunted under his breath at his hypocrisy. He was more open with his emotions than he'd been raised to be, but when he was uncomfortable, he could shut it down like a pro.

"William," his mother said with a smile as they

climbed the stairs. "What a lovely property Evie's mother has." *Like she wasn't familiar with it at all.* Jesus.

"I'm sure she'll be happy to hear that." He kissed her offered cheek, then turned and shook his father's hand. "How was the drive?"

"Uneventful." William McIntosh II extended his hand to the door. "Shall we?"

Liam took a deep breath. "Of course."

———

"Hey."

Evie kept staring straight ahead at her dresser as she pulled off her necklace and earrings, then stripped out of her sparkly blouse. They were finally home, Liam had just tucked the kids into bed, and she was bone tired. And upset.

Dinner had been fine. Evie's mother proved the perfect hostess to disarm Amelia McIntosh.

The two William McIntoshs, on the other hand…

"Evie." Liam clicked their bedroom door shut as he stepped inside. "*Evelyn.*"

She whirled around. "You're full naming me, *William?*"

"Sure am, Evelyn Calhoun. What's your problem? I thought we were all cool before dinner."

She narrowed her eyes. "Oooh, William McIntosh the third is being pokey, huh?"

He raised his brows, smirking a bit. "You want to pick a fight with me two nights before our wedding?"

"No, but I think the fight has picked itself."

He slowly undid the buttons on his dress shirt without saying anything else. Not engaging, she thought at first, but then she saw the warm burning ember of something else in his eyes. His fingers twisted each button loose—not just slowly, but strip-tease slowly.

He did look damn good in a suit. And even better peeling out of one. He kept talking as he bared his delicious skin, one slow, calm word at a time. "Tonight could have gone better."

"You think?" She threw her hands in the air. "Did you have to get into a fight with your father about monetary policy?"

He scrunched his face as if to say *oh well*.

"That, Liam! That's what I'm upset about!"

"On the upside, they love your mother's guest room."

"But you wouldn't care if they weren't happy." That anxious, panicky feeling rose in her chest again.

"I'd have cared. I promise. But tonight was just me and my dad butting heads. Nothing bigger."

She stared at him, torn between frustration and fatigue.

"Come here."

"No."

He laughed. "Why not?"

"You're going to make me forget why I'm grumpy." It would be pretty easy, actually.

"Sure am." He stripped off his shirt and met her at the foot of the bed. She stroked her hands over his bare torso. "I'm sorry."

"You should say you're sorry to your father. Or your mother, really."

"I should say a lot of things to my parents, but they're not here right now. They're not the most important person in my life. That's you, and right now, I'm sorry, to *you*. I let him get under my skin. I won't do it again this weekend, I promise."

"No debates about reasonable work hours or parenting techniques tomorrow?"

He nodded. "Cross my heart. And I'm taking Jess with me as my bodyguard when we have breakfast with them on Saturday morning."

"Good. I trust her." She laughed as he tickled up her ribs, but when he hooked his fingers under her bra straps and shoved them down her arms, baring her breasts, her giggles turned to sighs. "Liam..."

"We're getting married day after tomorrow."

"I know."

"I can't wait." He cupped one breast. "You're going to be my wife. We've got the most amazing family. You gave me that. You can be as mad as you want at me."

"I'm not mad," she said, her breath hitching. "I just worry."

He gazed down at her, a slight smile playing on his lips. "I keep telling you not to."

"But you don't," she whispered. "One of us has to care."

"I care about other things." He winked. "Like your orgasms."

Her sighs gave way to gasps as he dropped to his knees and kissed all over her torso, stroking her skin with light touches. She held his head to her chest, needing him to ease the heavy ache he'd just created.

"Your nipples are so hard," he whispered, his breath brushing across the sensitive peaks. "Begging to be pinched and sucked."

"Mmm, yes they are. You should do that."

"I will." Another gust of hot air as he circled one nipple with his tongue, open-mouthed. Her knees buckled, and he swept her off her feet, gently depositing her on the bed. While she watched from behind heavy, hooded eyelids, instantly feeling drugged on the promise of Liam inside her, he stripped out of his dress pants, then removed hers as well.

"This is how we should have all of our fights. Naked."

"Were we fighting?" she asked, as he resumed his attention on her breasts. Between their bodies, his erection pressed insistently against her belly.

"Exactly."

6
______

EVIE woke up early the day before the wedding and went for a run. That was Liam's first clue that something was still nagging at her, because Evie preferred almost all other forms of exercise, but she just kissed him sweetly when she came back, then took the kids to school and daycare before disappearing to a spa in Exeter for the morning. She took her sister and Jess with her, and when they got back, looking pretty much as they had when they left, just a bit shinier—for a guy who grew up hearing constantly about spa visits, he still didn't quite get the appeal—she still didn't give him any clue as to what might be on her mind.

She pulled out her clipboard, which Jess immediately snatched from her and started reading off the printed *One Day To Go Checklist*. Everything was done.

They called Beth on speakerphone and double checked that everything was done on her end.

"Totally under control. Looking forward to having forty-five of your closest friends and family in the Wine Cellar for dinner tonight. Chef just told me the prime rib will be medium rare, and the salmon looks amazing, it just arrived fresh on ice from the supplier."

"And we've got a microphone? I know the DJ will have one tomorrow, but I think there will be speeches tonight." Evie worried her bottom lip.

"Stella has already set up the A/V equipment." Beth's confidence rolled through the air. "We're good to go for tonight, Evie, enjoy this afternoon."

Once they hung up, Evie fluttered her hands in the air. "Okay. We're really just...everything's done."

Jess laughed. "You've worked hard planning this wedding."

Evie jumped up. "Maybe I should make some lunch."

Liam snagged her wrist. "Maybe Jess should make some lunch. Come with me for a minute."

He dragged her into their bedroom, closing the library door on the way through to give them extra privacy. Their new master suite jutted into the backyard, off the back of the house, behind the nursery. They were, for all intents and purposes, alone.

He tugged her hard against his body, squeezing her ass with one hand and the nape of her neck with the other. He took her mouth before she could protest, sliding his tongue along hers in a possessive, determined way.

"You need to get out of your head," he muttered, rocking against her. "Get some of those good feeling endorphins pumping through your system."

She whimpered as he pushed her lips open again, stealing her breath so she couldn't protest as he undid her jeans.

"I'm going to make you come, Evie. I'm going to lick you until you want to scream."

"You're crazy," she said, chasing his mouth for another kiss before he lay her back onto the bed, laying her out like a feast for his eyes and hands and mouth, then dropped to his knees and peeled off her panties.

———

Evie squirmed as Liam pressed her legs open. He stroked his fingertips lightly over her sensitive, freshly-bared skin.

"I'm starting to see the appeal of spa days," he said, kissing his way up her right thigh. "Is it sensitive?"

"No," she whispered. "Touch me."

"Take your shirt off." His words were low and rough. Demanding. She licked her lips and did as she was told, loving the dark approval in his eyes.

She was always wet for him—because he worked

her like a finely tuned violin—but this was on a different level. Arousal scratched hot beneath her skin, and she rocked her hips toward his mouth.

Apparently being greedy for licks turned Liam on. In the blink of an eye, he shifted from teasing and caring to demanding and hungry.

Sometimes when he went down on her, it felt like a long, slow, sexy kiss. Today he went straight for the sex, thrusting his tongue into her, then swiping up to her clit, rocking her to the edge of darkness already before sliding deep again, his mouth hot and open, insistent on consuming her entire sex. Over and over again he devoured her until she started trembling and covered her mouth with her arm to keep from crying out. Then he flipped her over, covered her body with his, and slid what felt like an impossibly large erection between her folds.

"Yes," she whispered, lifting her ass into the air. "Yes, yes, yes."

"You feel so good," he muttered against her ear as he dragged himself out of her, only to surge deep again, filling her. Stretching her.

She moaned and spread her legs wider still, wanting more of that stretch. Wanting him as deep as she could get him.

"And you're all mine, forever." He nipped at the curve of her ear, his breath hot and hitching. "I'm going to fill you with my babies, over and over again. I'm never going to get enough of your sweetness."

Her eyes were closed, but she could feel the darkness edging in. Breathing deep, she tried to hold on, not wanting to be done yet. She'd never get enough of him, either. His hands on her body, his words in her ear. Inside, she squeezed around him and he shuddered.

"Mine," he ground out, rearing up on his knees a bit. His mouth drifted to the top of her spine, then she felt the press of his forehead there as he arched above her, his hands gripping her hips. He was watching himself drive into her body.

"Yours," she panted, and on the next thrust, she gasped and gave in to the delicious blank of her orgasm, where nothing mattered but the contraction deep inside her body, then the stuttering ripples out to her extremities.

Liam muttered her name in a strangled whisper as he pulled out, spilling himself on her back.

"Oh my God," she whispered. That had been incredible, and she still ached for more of him.

"You okay?" he asked breathlessly in her ear as he stroked a soft cloth down her spine.

"Mmmm." She nodded. Her thighs throbbed, and she wasn't sure if she wanted to press them together or spread herself out wantonly.

He rolled her over again, staying on his knees above

her, and she started laughing. "You're still dressed." She hadn't even noticed his jeans bumping against her legs.

"And you're not." He lazily perused her naked body, and she stretched under his gaze. "Evie?"

"Hmmm?"

"Are you still turned on?"

"Maybe."

Ever so slowly, he dropped himself on top of her, clothes and all, and when he was nose-to-nose with her, he licked her bottom lip. "Then we need to do something about that."

"What do you have in mind?" she whispered.

"I want to kiss that pretty pussy of yours again, sunshine." He rolled onto his back and tugged her on top of him. "Slide that sweet ass of yours up here and show me what's mine."

"Yours," she whispered, rising above him, shifting closer, and then closer still as he wrapped his hands around her thighs, positioning them on either side of his face.

This time, instead of darkness she just saw the brightest light when she came, riding his fingers and rocking against his mouth as he sucked her clit. And when she was done, he rolled them both under the blankets and held her close.

"You think they've given up on us joining them for lunch?" she finally whispered.

"Probably." He laughed gently and tucked an errant

lock of hair behind her ear. "Hey...now that we've used up some of that anxious energy, do you want to talk about last night?"

Evie twisted her fingers in the bed sheet and sighed. "No. I let my feelings get all invested, even though I know it's silly."

"Know what's silly?"

She turned her head to look at him. "Jess and I got into the wine the other night and talked about you. She said some things that made a lot of sense, and they've been percolating in my head ever since."

A guarded look dropped over his face, and she mentally kicked herself for doing this today.

"Never mind."

"No..." He exhaled heavily. "I can admit that I don't like to talk about my parents. But we're a team. If you're worrying about this, then I need to be concerned as well."

"Yeah?"

He nodded. "What did my ever-so-wise friend say?"

Evie laughed, then took a deep breath. "She thinks I'm trying to repair your relationship with your parents by making everything perfect. That if it's good enough, they'll... I don't know. It's silly when I say it out loud."

"It's not silly." He stroked her cheek. "You're missing part of the puzzle, though."

"What part?"

"The thing about my parents...about my entire

family, really, is everything needing to be perfect? That's what broke me in the first place. I'm not that guy."

"But you *are* perfect! I don't get why they don't see that."

He laughed. "You've got it backwards, sunshine. *I* don't see myself as perfect. Because I'm not, right? I'm perfect for you, like you're perfect for me, but I've got my faults. And my parents can't see that. Literally, instead of embracing me warts and all, they just choose not to see all the ways I'm not what they want me to be. That creates a lot of blind spots."

"And you're just okay with that?" Evie couldn't imagine not wanting to throttle her mother if the situation were reversed. She wanted to shake Liam's parents and say, *see him! He's beautiful and kind and strong and brave!*

"I've lived with those parameters for my entire life." He pulled her closer, until their faces were touching. Focusing was kind of hard, but maybe that was the idea, because Liam never opened up like this. If he needed to be so close everything was blurry and almost not real, she could handle it. Even if she really, really wanted to see his whole face right now, and for him to see hers. "I didn't know how much bigger love could be until I met you."

"They love you." Evie believed that to the depth of her soul. "I know your mom struggles, but she keeps trying."

"Nobody loves me like you do. And I love that you expect them to." He pressed his forehead against hers so tightly it almost hurt. "I love you so much. I know I don't say it as much as I should, but I do. I can't wait to stand up in front of everyone we know tomorrow and tell you all the million reasons why."

She blinked back tears that weren't allow to fall. "I love you, too. I never doubt your love, you know. You show it so well."

He kissed her then, slow and open and sweet until it tripped back into breathtakingly hot, and then being so close they felt like one person, Liam fit himself between her legs and made it truly so. This time she came quickly, the echo of those three little words ringing in her ears.

7

HER first wedding morning had been spent at her parents' farm, but Ava slept better in her own room, so this time Evie woke up in the bed she shared with Liam—and had shared with him the night before, which made her smile. He'd left a half hour earlier, but she'd stayed in bed, enjoying the butterflies in her tummy and thinking about the day to come.

Liam was off to breakfast with his parents. They would either come to be cool with him as he was, because there was no chance of Liam turning into the man they wanted him to be—too bad for them, because Evie loved the man he was. Or they might not, she thought sadly. And he'll find a way to open up them, or he won't. But either way, Evie couldn't fix their relationship or make any of that different than what it was because it wasn't her problem. That realization was freeing.

Besides, it was her wedding day. No expense had been spared, no detail left unworried. Now she got to enjoy all that hard work.

Liam left their bedroom door open when he left, and in the quiet of the empty house she heard Ava roll over in the next room, then pull herself up to stand against the crib rail. Evie could picture her sleepily looking around, wondering where all the usual noise had gone. *It's just us, girlie. A little treat.* As her baby let out her first tentative cry, she rolled out of bed.

"Morning, my precious," she said as she padded into the nursery.

"Uh!" Ava waved her arms in the air.

"Yep, up you get, birthday girl. Come on, let's get dressed." After a quick snuggle, Evie put her daughter in grey leggings and a pink t-shirt that said *Flowergirl*, then carried her back to the master bedroom. She plunked the toddler in the middle of the bed and put on her own matching outfit, black leggings and a grey t-shirt that said *Wifey*. "Your aunt should be arriving any second with your brothers—"

Right on schedule, the front door cracked open, and Max's winter boots hit the floor with a heavy thud as he whipped them off.

She dashed into living room. "Boots in the closet,

please! We're going to have a lot of people in and out this morning."

"Hi, Mom."

"Hey my darlings." They'd slept at Kyle and Laney's renovated school house the night before, which hadn't really been necessary, but she'd appreciated the alone time with Liam. Tomorrow morning they were going to their dad's for four days, so she felt a pang of sadness about the extra day apart, but they looked happy for the sleepover with their aunt and uncle—two people they didn't see nearly as often.

"Uncle Kyle dropped us off. His truck is really cool."

"I know!" She laughed as they tumbled into the living room, spreading their stuff everywhere. "Closet! Oh for Pete's sake."

From behind her boys, her sister waved a bottle of champagne. "Never mind, I brought mimosa makings!"

Evie squinted. "You're missing orange juice."

"Ooops." Laney winked. "No, just kidding. Carrie's right behind me with the rest of the breakfast stuff."

Sure enough, right behind her was the curvy, effervescent redhead with an overflowing picnic basket. Pretty soon the hairdresser and make-up artist were there, Maroon 5 was blaring, and everyone was dancing. Evie took a quick picture of Ava and sent it Liam. **Your girls are having fun. Hope you are too!**

They didn't have a big wedding party, just Laney as

her attendant and Jess as Liam's, and the kids, but she did have a lot of wonderful friends, and over the morning they all came by, even Karen and her gorgeous three-day-old baby boy. Evie had a wee snuggle with him while the make-up artist gave Karen a free "new mom" makeover.

Stella Nixon, Carrie's cousin and Evie's part-time help at the Pilates studio arrived with her best friend, Mari Beadie, while Evie's hair was being straightened into shiny, perfect almost waves. They both looked sexy as sin in little black dresses, and promised to dance all night.

By noon, all their friends were gone, and the photographer had arrived, and right behind him was Evie's mother.

"I'm sorry I couldn't get here earlier," she said, pressing a quick kiss to Evie's cheek. "Had some things to do."

"What things?" Evie desperately wanted to get her wedding clipboard, but Jess had stolen it before the rehearsal dinner and swore nothing else needed to be worried about.

"Oh, you know." Claire waved her hands in the air.

"No, I don't. You didn't have any assigned tasks today."

Laney giggled.

"Shut up, you've had too much wine." Evie frowned. "Is everything okay, Mom?"

"Of course." Claire smiled brightly. "Seriously, every-thing is perfect."

Before Evie could ask any more questions, the photographer was nudging her toward the bedroom to put on her dress. Laney followed, making happy claps the whole way.

"This is so fun, all the wedding happiness without any of the planning stress."

"Says the eloper."

"I know, aren't we clever?" Laney gasped at the sight of the dress hanging from the curtain rod. "Oh, Evie!"

She'd gone back and forth on what to wear so many times, but finally decided that even though this was her second wedding, and she was as far from a virgin as possible, it didn't matter. She didn't want this wedding to be any less significant than her first one.

"It's pretty?"

"My wedding dress was pretty. This is stunning." Laney's voice went all breathy, and she sighed as she touched the silk organza dress. It was strapless, with a tight bodice to a natural waist, highlighted with an ivory silk ribbon. And from there, a million acres of layered organza, floaty and magical.

"Ava has a tiny version of it. It's totally ridiculous. And nobody has seen either of them, it's been my little secret."

"Wow." Laney took a deep breath. "Nope, not ridiculous. It's perfect. You deserve to be a princess for a day, Ev."

The photographer took a few pictures of her dress and her shoes, then she was left alone to slip into her pale blue lingerie before they came back in and got her buttoned up.

Back in the living room, Evie's mother had dressed Connor and Max in their suits in record time.

Connor stepped forward first. "You're super pretty, Mom."

Evie reached out her hand, grateful that he took it. Both the compliment and the willing touch were so rare these days. "And you're so handsome, so very grown-up. Look at you."

"Are you going to cry?"

She smiled. "Maybe. Let me guess, that wouldn't be cool?"

"Not cool at all. But it's okay. Both Dad and Liam told me you would, and I shouldn't tease you about it."

"Your dad said that?" Her smile got bigger. Her relationship with Dale had improved greatly over the last year, but the thoughtfulness still surprised her.

"He also said it was a lot of money to spend on a party."

Okay, so the magnanimous thoughts only went so far. "Well, it is. But it's an important day for Liam and me. And a lot of people helped us make it really special."

"We know," Max interjected, sliding in beside his brother.

"Shhh," Connor said.

"What's going on?" She looked back and forth between her kids.

Connor shook his head. "We can tell you when it's time to go, and not a minute sooner."

She narrowed her gaze. "Is this like the bed and breakfast plan? Am I going to like this?"

Max nodded. "Liam said it's perfect."

She laughed. "That probably means no, but I'll be wrong. Okay. Let's go wake your sister up from her nap, yes? And take some pictures before you get all wrinkled from wrestling?"

———

"Message from your bride?"

His mother's voice broke through Liam's thoughts, and he glanced up from his phone. He'd been pretty good about not having it out during brunch, but they were back at the Calhoun farm now. Claire had already left for Evie's house, but he and Jess were going to get ready there in a silly nod to tradition that he shouldn't see the bride before the ceremony. "A picture of Ava dancing."

"Can I see?"

"Of course." He handed over the phone and glanced

at the wall clock, distracted. "You can scroll to the right or left to see more."

She settled into the arm chair beside the wood stove.

He paced into the hallway and raised his voice, projecting up the stairs. "Jess? We should go soon."

"The ceremony isn't for an hour yet, but sure, let's go stand in the cold for a while." His friend appeared at the top of the stairs, looking extra pretty in a black dress.

"Where is my boutonniere?" he asked.

"In the living room." She said the words patiently, like maybe they'd already had this conversation. He followed her to the front of the house, away from where his mother still sat with his phone. "Where is your father? There's one for him, as well, and bouquets for myself and your mother."

"He's on a conference call. We'll leave their flowers here."

She reached out and grabbed his arm. "Liam."

"What?"

"Go give your mother her flowers, you knob."

"Oh." Right. He picked up the box and headed back to the kitchen.

"Mom?"

She looked up with a bright smile. "Your kids are all so photogenic."

He put the box down on the kitchen table and sat on the ottoman next to her. "They are."

"Max has such a strong sense of humour. But

Connor...I can see your influence on him. He'll go far in life."

"Unlike me?" The barb slipped out before he could stop it.

"Oh, Liam." She shook her head. "Don't be ridiculous."

"You're right. Today's not the day for that."

She frowned. "No. Of course it's not, but that's not what I meant." She pressed her carefully lined lips together. "You've always gone your own way. I had my doubts, but I was wrong. You've ended up with a wonderful woman."

On that point, they could agree. "Thank you."

"Are you nervous about today?"

He shook his head. Distracted, yes. Nervous...not a chance in hell. "I can't wait."

"Then go. I still remember waiting outside the church when I married your father, watching people arrive from behind the tinted glass of the limousine."

"Yeah?"

She nodded. "Let Jessica wait inside, because it's cold, but you should go and greet your guests as they arrive."

He leaned in and gave her a less perfunctory than usual kiss on the cheek. "Thank you. Again."

At the church, they found the minister talking to Beth Stewart in the entrance way.

"Lovely day to get married, Liam." Pastor Branton

strode forward with an outstretched hand.

"Sunny day, bit of snow, not too cold. Couldn't ask for a better Valentine's Day wedding."

"You know, I didn't ask you two...whose idea was that?"

Liam laughed. "Once Evie insisted on waiting until our lives settled down, it became the obvious choice. Today also happens to be our daughter's first birthday."

"Two parties in one."

"Something like that."

"You're here earlier than I expected."

"I got some unexpected advice from my mother, and decided to take it."

The minister laughed. "Sounds about right."

A clap on his back interrupted their conversation. Liam turned and accepted a handshake from Finn Howard, Beth's husband. "You good to go, man?"

"Sure am."

"I've got a flask, if you need a shot for courage."

"I'm good." He took a deep breath. "But maybe a shot for calm?"

They stepped outside just in time to see Evan West arrive with his date, a tall, blonde man named Adam. Evan made the introductions, and then they all had a toast to Evie.

Over the next half hour, it was a constant stream of people. Chase Miller and Mari Beadie, who reassured him all was set for the reception. Stella Nixon was with them. Ty West arrived on his own, but lingered outside until Stella went to find a seat.

Those two should go on a date, Liam thought. The last thing he needed to do was play matchmaker, but the mutual attraction was obvious.

The last guests to arrive were those with children. Ian and Carrie Nixon, with their two kids. Paul Reynolds and Karen Miller, with their baby boy sleeping in his bucket car seat, and the proudest older sister Liam had ever seen, Megan Reynolds.

He gave Karen a quick hug and told her she looked beautiful. She really did, motherhood agreed with her.

His parents arrived, and he slowly escorted them up the aisle, accepting handshakes every few feet. When he showed them to their seats in the front row, his father was still stiff and remote, but his mother seemed moved.

And then Jess was at his elbow, directing him to his spot.

It was time.

He was more than ready.

Evie had hired a string trio for the ceremony, and they'd been playing since he'd arrived. Now they paused, and as the minister gave them their cue, they started a new song. Pachelbel's *Canon in D major*. How many weddings had he heard this piece at? It was pretty. Traditional. Expected.

And for the first time, it affected him to his very core.

The doors has been closed as he made his way up

the aisle, but now they opened again, slowly, and around the corner peeked Ava.

And then she disappeared.

He grinned. Saved by the adorable toddler, the tears that might have threatened melted into pure joy.

When she peeked out again, he held out his hand, and she toddled toward him, dropping her flower basket not far into her long journey down the aisle.

Behind her, her brothers came, solemnly and carefully.

Then Laney, pretty in blue, and when she got to the dropped flower basket, she picked it up and started scattering the flower petals her niece had abandoned.

Liam's grin got bigger.

And finally there was his partner in crime. His lover, his best friend, and his soon-to-be wife.

She floated forward, the bright winter sun from the foyer backlighting her, casting a glow through the veil that hung from the crown of her hair, down her back, and behind her to the floor.

Gorgeous wasn't the right adjective, although she was. Breathtaking. Magnificent. Perfect.

And *his*.

Her eyes sparkled as she joined him, her fingers sliding over his as he tugged her close.

"Hey," she said on a breath, then grinned.

"Hey. Want to get married?"

"More than anything."

$$8$$

THE ceremony started with a prayer, then Kyle read *i carry your heart* by e.e. cummings, and the whole time Liam grinned at her like this was the most awesome thing in the world.

It really was.

After a brief introduction from the minister, the part of the ceremony Evie was most looking forward to began.

Like her dress, their vows were a surprise to each other. Liam had resisted the idea of matching vows, not wanting to use something canned, so she'd given him that win.

"I'm a deeds, not words kind of guy." Liam paused and she smiled at him, tremulously. *It's okay*, she said with her eyes. *I know.* "But I knew today would be the day to say all the words. And since that's hard, I started early. More than a year ago, I asked you to marry me, Evie. And almost every day since then, I've made a note in my phone about something I want to include in my vows."

She stared at him, wide-eyed, as he pulled that phone from his pocket.

"I know, sunshine. No phones. Totally gauche. What would my mom say?" That was met by an unexpected giggle from the front row, and Evie twisted just enough to see Amelia wiping her eyes, her lips pressed together to hold back further laughter. Everyone else joined her, a ripple of amusement waving through the room, and Evie turned back to her love. He winked. "I think she'd say that you're worth breaking all the rules. So here we go. Ready? I'm not going to list all of them, but we're going to be here for a while."

"Oh my God," Evie said, happy tears threatening.

The minister cleared his throat and Evie winced in apology.

"January 6th. She's thirty-five weeks pregnant and wakes up early every morning to make her boys oatmeal from scratch. February 14th. Best day of my life, hands down. This woman is stronger than strong." He took a deep breath, not looking at her, but then he peeked up from his phone and flashed a bright smile. One tear slipped down her cheek, but she barely noticed.

"March 11th. She's been pacing with Ava for at least two hours, bouncing up and down, up and down. She's never been more beautiful. April 19th. Candlelight dinner complete with dessert. How lucky am I? June 2nd. A note in my lunchbox." Liam paused and looked up. They both remembered that note. It had been x-rated, and he'd come home and then scarfed that lunch in a hurry on his way back to work after spending most of the hour naked.

I love you, she mouthed, and he echoed the silent promise before continuing.

"July 1st. Canada Day breakfast—make our own ice cream sundaes. The sacrifices she makes for me." Another laugh. He was definitely winning the vows today, hers paled in comparison. She was totally okay with that.

"August 22. Stopped by the studio and just watched her work at the counter for a few minutes before she saw me at the window. I'm so proud of the business she's built. October 7th. She gives the best hugs. November 29th. Dark stormy day, and there's my sunshine. Blonde shining hair, spinning around in the circle as she dances with our kids. December 24th. One year ago, I asked her to marry me. Smartest thing I ever did. December 25th. And she has great taste in presents. January 11th. Made me drink something bright green because I'm sick. January 12th. Not sick anymore."

Liam paused for everyone to finish laughing, then he

tucked his phone away and reached for her hands. "And February 14th, here we are again. I think in all of that I forgot to actually say some vows, so I'll just make it easy. You're my everything, Evie. I love you with all of my heart, and I vow that everything I have and everything I am is forever yours."

The minister turned to her, then paused and handed over a tissue. Everyone laughed again as she took it. Liam held on to her other hand the whole time, and after she'd sorted herself out, she tipped her face to the ceiling and sucked in a slow, measured breath before starting.

"Liam, you're my better half in every way. You're calm to my fire and you bring logic to my crazy ideas. You always believe in me, and I also think *you* give the best hugs. That's convenient. You're an amazing father and step-father, and for all of that, I love you so very much. Today, I give myself to you as your wife, but you've already proved to be the most excellent husband. I promise in front of God, our family, and all of our friends to love you with all of my heart, for the rest of my life. I'll be the fire to your calm, and bring a little crazy to your logic. And I'll always believe in you."

Liam tipped his head forward, almost touching their foreheads, and smiled. She thought for a second he'd skip to the end and just kiss her right then, but then he glanced to the side at her sons, and wiggled his head.

"And now the groom is going to make a separate vow

to Connor and Max," said the minister, explaining to both Evie and the audience what was happening.

Evie stared at her boys as they approached, grinning. "Did you guys plan this?" she asked.

They nodded vigorously as Liam knelt to look them in the eye. Evie reached blindly behind her and either the minister or Laney slid another tissue into her hand. Wedding dresses really need pockets, she thought. Or built in handkerchiefs.

"Connor and Max," Liam started. "First of all, thank you for letting me marry your mom. I love her a lot. And I love you guys, too. I promise to be a fair step-dad, and always respect the relationship you have with your mom and your dad. I promise to be a friend when you need one, and a grown-up when you need one. And when we fight about which one I need to be at a given time, well... we can hash that out over ice cream. Deal?" They both nodded, and he held out his hand first to Connor, then to Max, solemnly shaking their hands before pulling them in for a hug, which had Ava squealing and running over from the front row to get in on the family love, so Evie knelt to join them all, too.

It took a few kisses, but the kids all returned to their spots and Liam helped Evie to stand again.

The exchange of rings, signing of the registry, and final prayer flitted by in a blur. She almost missed the musicians playing Bach's *Air on The G String* during the signing, but then she remembered as Laney and Jess put their signatures on the various papers. She bumped arms with Liam, and he wiggled his eyebrows. Yeah, he remembered how much she'd giggled when she chose that piece of music.

Time slowed again as they took their places in front of the congregation again. Pastor Branton covered their hands with his, waited a beat, then pronounced them husband and wife.

And then the world just stopped. They'd really done it. Liam—her one-night stand, her younger man, her way-out-of-her-league fantasy—was her husband. And he was *beaming* at her.

No Wardham girl was ever this lucky. She must be dreaming.

"My wife," Liam said, sliding his arms around her waist. Nope, not dreaming. She let out a little gasp as he braced her hips with one hand and tipped her to the side, his other palm sliding across the bare skin beneath her hair. His mouth covered hers in a searing brand, a kiss that declared their union in no uncertain terms.

Two more kisses followed once he had her upright again, both of his hands cupping her face.

"My wife," he repeated, pride rippling off him, and she pressed up on her toes, giving him one kiss of her own.

Only then did she realize that everyone in the church was on their feet, cheering and clapping. And hooting. She could feel her cheeks turning red, but

Liam's fingers tangled with hers and then she didn't care.

He picked up Ava and she held Max's hand, who held Connor's hand, and as a family they headed for the door. It was time to party.

9

THE wedding reception didn't officially start until half past five, because they had enough farmer friends like Ian Nixon who needed to do afternoon chores between the church and the rest of the celebration at the winery.

But most people made their way there pretty quickly, and by the time Liam, Evie, and the kids finished up with the formal wedding photography, they found a happy party waiting for them in the tasting room.

The original plan had been to hold the dinner reception in the dining room of the inn, to be a bit different from the rehearsal dinner the night before, but the way that everyone had made themselves at home in the main building, Liam saw another silver lining to the change in plans.

Beth had outdone herself with decorating, using just

enough touches of red and pink to nod at the holiday without overwhelming.

After entering together, Liam went one direction and Evie went the other, greeting all of their guests, but his gaze never strayed from his wife for long.

He was glad to sit for dinner, to get to hold her hand and talk quietly between speeches. Evan deftly guided the party toward the evening of dancing, right on schedule.

"I've got a surprise for you," Liam whispered to Evie as Mari went over to talk to the DJ. Liam knew she'd stashed her guitar and an amp behind the table, he just needed to keep his wife distracted for a minute while their songstress friend set up on the small stage.

He pulled Evie in close for a chaste kiss, but lingered a bit long. He couldn't help himself. She tasted like champagne.

"Nice surprise?"

He laughed and tipped his head. "Not the kiss. Her."

Evie gasped and clapped her hands together. "A song! Oh, yay!"

Everyone in the room swivelled their gaze to the stage as Mari started talking in the mic. "What a wonderful day for a wedding!" She nodded as everyone clapped. "I tend to sing songs about grumpy men, and for all of Liam's interesting characteristics, being grumpy isn't one of them. Besides, today's a day to cele-brate love. And to do that right, I'd really need to sing long songs. That puts me in a pickle, because I don't tend to write those. No offence, sweetie."

Chase Miller tipped his beer at his fiancée and smiled.

Mari continued. "Now, Liam told me that Evie's favourite song is a country tune, a little romantic ballad called 'Hold Me In Your Arms'. I quite like it, too, and in fact I had the opportunity to meet Bren Getson last summer at a folk festival in Hamilton." She paused there and looked down at her guitar with a secret smile that made Liam proud. Beside him, Evie had her head tipped to the side, her hand pressed to her chest.

She looked touched.

Ha. She was about to have her mind blown.

Mari looked up and started strumming her guitar quietly, the first few swaying notes of the love song. "So when I called him and asked him to stop by Wardham this weekend for the wedding of the century, of course he said yes. Ladies and gentlemen, Mr. Bren Getson."

From the back of the room, a rich, masculine voice filled the space. The up-and-coming Canadian country music singer sang the first chorus of the song as he approached the head table. He stopped in front of Evie, winked at her, then joined Mari on the stage.

Under the table, Evie's other hand gripped Liam's leg as tears popped into her eyes.

He wrapped his arm around her shoulders and they

swayed back and forth in their chairs to the liquid silk of the perfectly harmonized song.

As the song came to a slow, crooning end, Bren nodded to the applauding room, then talked quietly with Mari for a second before looking to the head table. "Mari has informed me that your first dance song is 'I Don't Dance' by Lee Brice. It just so happens my wife loves that song, so if you want to step onto the dance floor..."

Faster than lightning, Evie was out of her chair, then she spun back for Liam, much to everyone's delight. He took her hand with a wink. The sexy singer could get her all excited, but unlike Mr. Brice, Liam *could* dance, so he confidently led her onto the dance floor, knowing soon her entire attention would be back on him.

Grazing his hand over her hip, careful to avoid snagging her veil or the cloud-like layers of her dress, he stepped her back, then spun her slowly as the song started, enjoying the smile on her face.

"We did it," she whispered.

"No dramas."

"You did make all of our guests go to the church in school buses."

"Make is such a strong word, sweetheart." He winked. "The transportation was provided for anyone who wanted it. They were welcome to drive their fancy cars if they'd rather."

"I hear there was hot apple cider and blankets on the buses. People seemed to like that."

"I can't take full credit for the idea." Or any, but he had approved it. Maybe he had a little of that executive DNA in him after all.

"Who suggested it?"

He laughed as he stepped them sideways, then turned a slow circle, loving the way she swayed in his arms. "The buses? That was Max. And the cider and blankets was Evan."

"Speaking of my first boyfriend..." Her lips quirked as she said that. "He asked if I'd do a dance with him since my dad is gone. If you want to dance with your mom, I mean. And if you don't mind."

He raised his eyebrows. "I think you're underestimating my ego and the level of pride I take in keeping you satisfied. Of course you can dance with Evan."

———

A LITTLE OVER A YEAR AGO, they'd stood at the edge of this very same dance floor, watching the party swirl around them, and when Evan had asked her to dance *then*, Liam had urged her to do it, but his words had had a certain bite.

He was right. He had all the confidence in the world in the security of their relationship, because it was good and healthy.

"I love you so much, Liam McIntosh. You fill me with joy."

"That's not all I'm going to fill you with. I've got another surprise for the end of the night."

She blinked up at him. "You didn't just..."

"I did." He smirked.

"I love you."

"Are you just saying that to remind yourself now?"

She laughed and threw her arms around his neck as the song came to an end. He hugged her tight, lifting her off the ground and twirling her around in a circle.

Max and Connor waylaid her on the way to dance with Evan, but he didn't look like he minded, so she twirled with her boys, and then Ava too as Laney brought her over, while Liam danced with his mother. Then the DJ took over, and she got a chance to thank Bren Getson in person.

"Would you like to stay and have a drink?" she offered.

"That's lovely and kind of you, Evie, but I've got my own wife to get back to. I've been on the road for a month now and she's flying into Detroit tonight."

"Well, thank you so much. This was such a lovely surprise." She beamed, then turned to Mari as soon as he was gone and squealed. "Oh my God. Bren Getson? You've been holding out on me."

Mari shrugged. "I didn't know you were a fangirl until Liam told me. And while I know Bren, I have to be honest, it was the promise of Chase showing up for a fundraiser in the summer that cinched the deal."

"You kiss that man for me."

"Will do." They shared another squeal, then headed back to the dance floor.

After an hour of partying, Ava started yawning, so Evie sat down with her at the side of the room and rubbed her back for a couple of minutes until she fell asleep. When she'd started looking for a place to stash the snoozing toddler, Liam's mother and Aunt Edith waved her over. Slowly, to keep from waking the sleeping kid, she joined them.

"You can put her on a blanket here, if you want. We're not going to dance all night like you are," Amelia said.

"Really?"

"Of course. I know I'm not the most maternal person, but I can watch my sleeping granddaughter for a couple hours. I'll use her to lure people who might otherwise be afraid to talk to me."

Evie's mouth dropped open. "Uhhhh..."

Edith laughed. "She's kidding."

Amelia mock-scowled at her sister-in-law. "Shhh, don't give away all my secrets."

Evie carefully kneeled on the floor, tucking Ava carefully between two chairs in clear sight of her guardians. "Thank you."

She stood to leave them to their conversation, but Amelia reached out and touched her arm. "Evie, wait."

"Yes?" Her heart thumped in her chest.

"Thank you."

"For what?"

"For loving my son. For understanding him in a way I never could."

Evie smiled. "He makes it easy for me."

Amelia shook her head. "Give yourself more credit than that. He's always been his own person. Restless, too. But with you, he's found his home."

Yeah, he had. Evie grinned, then leaned forward and kissed her mother-in-law. "Well, thank *you*."

"Now go dance. You're too beautiful to not be the centre of attention."

On her way back to the dance floor, she went to the bar, looking for water. There she found Evan, looking unexpectedly glum.

"You okay?"

He looked at her in surprise. "Oh, of course. It's one of my best friends' wedding. It's a wonderful day."

"I'm sorry we didn't get a dance earlier, do you want to now?"

He wrinkled his face at the dance music that had drawn everyone else onto the floor. "I'm good."

"What's going on?"

"You're like a dog with a bone, aren't you?"

"I'm a mom. We can sniff bullshit at a hundred yards."

He stared across the room for a minute before sighing and looking down at his hands clenched tight around a beer. "I'm feeling guilty for being a terrible date."

"Adam?" The rower had seemed nice. Young. Athletic. Not overly bright, but yummy to look at. "What happened?"

"He wanted to go away for a weekend."

"And you wanted to…"

"Work."

"Ouch."

"And then there's…" Again his gaze drifted across the room, and this time, she followed. He was looking at Jess. "Nothing."

"Evan." Evie leaned in and lowered her voice. "It's okay to like girls, you know."

His jaw clenched. "If only it were that simple."

"I don't know. I thought my life was a lot more complicated than it was. All I had to do was trust Liam."

"And what about if I'm the one that nobody can trust? Hmm?" He tipped his glass back, draining the contents before thudding it heavily on the bar. "It doesn't matter who I'm attracted to, Evie. The truth is, I'm always going to eventually want someone else."

She watched helplessly as her friend turned and disappeared behind a crowd of people. He was right…

tonight hadn't been the best time for that conversation. But when she got back from her honeymoon, they were going to have lunch. He was a good guy, and deserved to be happy. Maybe there was a way she could help him figure out what he truly wanted in a life partner.

10

____

BY midnight, the party was winding down. The boys stayed up to the bitter end, then happily packed off with their aunt and uncle for one more night of sleepover. They'd see them again for brunch before leaving for the mini-honeymoon, but Evie still felt oddly clingy as she hugged them both goodbye.

Ava went home with all of her grandparents, Claire promising that all would be fine. It would have to be, they were leaving her for three more nights.

"It's going to be okay," Liam whispered in her ear.

"What if it's not?" She twisted her face toward his.

"Then we'll go and pick her up. We have cell phones."

Evan was missing, but they said goodnight to everyone else as the last of the school buses pulled away to take people home. The buses would do a loop of the town. One nice thing about a town of just a few thousand people—there were only so many stops a bus would have to make before all major intersections had been covered.

"Ready to go?" Liam held up her pale blue velvet wrap.

"Sure am."

But when she took his hand, he didn't tug her in the direction of his car, parked nearby.

"Where are we going?"

He pointed to the inn. "To the honeymoon suite."

"Is that allowed? I thought Evan said the inn wasn't cleared for guests?"

"Well, I know the guy who renovated this place." And just to prove his point, the lights in the renovated mansion *were* on. There'd be no other reason for that.

Evie bit her lip. "So we have the whole place all to ourselves?"

"You can be as loud as you want," he murmured, holding the door open for her.

The suite was down the main hallway, not far from the vacant reception desk. Liam pulled a key from his pocket and opened the door. Inside, the bed was covered in rose petals and the gas fireplace was already going.

"Wow. You're just full of good surprises." She turned slowly in the space, then dropped her wrap on one of the arm chairs.

"Like I said, I know this guy..." Liam leaned back

against the door and crossed his arms, like he was happy just to watch her for a bit.

Two could tease. "Oh yeah? Does he have a tool belt? Because I have a thing for men all covered in saw dust."

"He might. Too bad you're mine now." He crooked his finger. She didn't move. This was fun.

"I'm yours?"

He crossed the room, slowly backing her up against the built-in bookcases. "All mine," he said softly, rubbing his nose along her cheek. "And I don't share with thugs in tool belts."

Her breath hitched in her chest. "Not even ones with wicked smiles and gorgeous eyes?"

"Sounds dangerous. You can never trust those guys."

"Maybe I only want a taste of him. Just a one-night stand."

He kissed along her neck, leaving a heavy ache of awareness everywhere he touched. "One-night stands can be dangerous, too."

"Oh?"

"He might take you hard. Over and over again. You'll use condoms like a good girl, but maybe you'll be too tempting, and he'll take you so hard the condom will rip."

"You think that's what would happen with me and my construction hero?"

His eyes flashed dark. "He's no hero. Just a regular guy."

"He's my hero. He came back to me."

"Luckiest day of his life."

"You looked like I'd punched you in the gut."

"Well, I was just hoping for a second date."

"That took a while."

"Worth waiting for." He stepped back. "How the hell do I get you out of this thing?"

She turned. "Buttons."

"Nice. Hands against the books."

She braced herself, smiling at the convenient position he'd chosen for unwrapping her and he made quick work of the long row of buttons, then the zipper underneath. Her dress puddled to the floor around her as Liam sucked in a breath.

Her lingerie was just that good.

"You like?" she asked, wiggling her hips.

"I'm starting to remember why I took you so hard that first night, all night long. Your ass in a thong..." He inhaled roughly as he stepped closer, carefully sliding his oxfords under her dress. So careful. So dirty. "It makes me lose control."

"I'm your wife," she whispered, looking at him over her shoulder. "You can do with me what you like."

He brushed her hair out of the way. "What happened to your veil?"

"I took it off hours ago, didn't you notice?"

"So much of today blurred right past."

"I know...hey, weren't you about to lose control?"

He pressed a kiss to her shoulder. "Can't. You're too precious to me."

"What if I ask very, very nicely?"

"How nicely?" Their faces were so close, they were almost kissing. His eyes glittered like onyx.

"Maybe nice is the wrong word." She licked her lips, almost licking his at the same time. "Sloppily. Greedily. On my knees."

With a growl, he kissed her, then turned her around and guided her to the floor, his hands heavy on her shoulders. She loved every second of it. Kneeling on her wedding dress, she watched, panting, as her husband unbuckled his belt.

She took him deep without her usual teasing preamble. Licking and kisses could be for the honeymoon. It was late, and this wasn't fun sex. It wasn't making love or being adventurous. This felt like *mating*. They were joining for a lifetime.

It could be desperate and urgent and intense.

Maybe it should be.

His hands settled on her head, encouraging her to swallow more of him than usual. And then he held her there.

Her womb clenched, and she moaned around him.

"So good," he whispered, easing her back, then doing it again. Twice more, then he shoved his shirt off and hauled her up his body, hoisting her into his arms. Tripping over his dress pants, he hopped sideways and they landed in a breathless pile on the bed. "Okay, so that was a little less suave."

She reached between and lazily fisted his cock . "This feels huge, right?"

He flexed against her palm.

"Not that." She squeezed to tell his erection it wasn't personal. "I mean tonight. Am I crazy?"

He shook his head. "No, I get it. I want to mark you as mine."

"I am yours."

His smile was slow, feral, and perfect. "I know."

He traced the edge of her bra, flipping one strap and then the other off her shoulders. She rolled onto her back as he continued his exploration of her body, and by the time he reached the edge of her panties, her body remembered the path his fingers were taking.

"That first night," she breathed.

"I wanted you so much it hurt. When you went back to your room, I decided if you didn't come back, I'd find a way to track you down."

"You changed my life that night. You with your sexy smile and fancy suit."

"When I took you home, I thought I'd never get another chance, so I wanted to commit your perfection to memory."

They continued like that, Liam touching all the parts of her that weren't soaking wet, trading secret memories of their first time. Then he slid her panties to the side, and the time for talking was over.

He went down on her first, licking up all the slippery evidence of how hot she'd found...everything.

When she came down from her first orgasm, he filled her up and gave her another, joining her this time.

Then they did it all over again, and when they were finally sore and tired and sated, Evie tucked her head under Liam's chin and sighed.

"What, sunshine? Need more?"

She smiled. "Soon. After a catnap."

"Then...."

"It's just that for months now, I've been planning today. And you've been secretly planning tonight. And tomorrow it'll all be over."

"Any time you want to wear that thong, I'm happy to book this room and we can do it all over again."

She kissed his chest and closed her eyes.

"Tomorrow's not the end of anything, Evie," he whispered. "It's just the start."

EPILOGUE

THEY didn't get to Pine Harbour until late in the afternoon, after brunch and an extended goodbye with the kids, but their arrival couldn't have been timed better—as they parked in front of the year-round cottage Finn Howard had arranged for them, the setting sun glinted through the soaring, snow-dusted pine trees that framed their view of Lake Huron.

"Wow," Evie said, leaning into her husband's side.

"That view was worth the drive." Liam pulled out his phone and held it away at an angle, taking a picture of first of them, then of the lake and the setting sun that lit it up in pinks and purples and greys.

"Happy honeymoon, my husband."

He winked at her and kissed her nose. "I'll grab the bags, you go see if the door is open. Finn said his brother would get it ready for us."

They were staying in the last cottage on the lane, closest to the lake. Across the road, there was another house, larger than the matching row of cottages, but built in the same style. All had large windows and spacious decks, and Evie already wanted to come back with the kids in the summer.

Where the house across the road was dark, this little one glowed—an oversized lantern-style outdoor light, lights on in the gourmet kitchen she could see through the windows, and on the far side of the cozy living room, a gas fireplace flickered.

And they were all alone.

Except the windows...maybe there were blinds.

She stepped inside, her eyes gobbling up all the little touches—a built-in wine rack, fully stocked with a little *Enjoy!* sign; slippers in a basket by the boot rack; a current newspaper on the breakfast bar.

"Where's the bedroom?"

Evie smiled at the sound of her new husband's voice and turned around, biting her lip playfully. "Who needs a bed when we're all alone?"

Liam's eyes danced, giving her a once-over as she peeled off her winter jacket. "I meant for the bags, but I like the way your mind is working."

"Oh, I haven't gotten that far yet. Probably down the hallway." She grabbed the bag of food they'd packed— and a quick kiss—as he made his way past.

They'd stopped for lunch on the way up, and

planned to find a diner for breakfast in the morning, but they'd packed a picnic of stuff for dinner. Olives, cheese, Italian salami, water crackers, marinated tomato salad, and chocolate-covered strawberries and cheesecake for dessert.

All decadent foodstuff that Evie never allowed herself to eat, but this was their honeymoon.

Her breath hitched in her throat as she remembered Liam's vows from the day before. She'd already known he was a good man. A wonderful father and partner, intent on providing for their growing family and being a steadfast support to her as she grew her own business.

She'd had no idea how *observant* he'd been the whole time. Pressing her fingers to her lips, she stepped away from the fridge and closed her eyes, leaning back against the counter as she replayed their wedding day in her head.

Liam standing tall and proud at the altar. How he held her as they were serenaded by her favourite country music singer—a wonderful surprise. The way he held Ava during pictures and included Connor and Max in the service.

How he'd undressed her in the honeymoon suite at the not-yet-open Go West Inn. Remembering the intense physical connection they'd shared—as good as always, but extra-special because of the vows they'd just exchanged—a warm heat pulsed through Evie's lower belly.

She felt another warmth, this one just about six feet tall, slide against her.

"What are you thinking about?" Liam murmured as he wrapped his arms around her, one hand stroking over her neck and up into her hair, the other settling on her far hip.

"You," she said quietly, twisting into the hard, hot length of his body. He'd taken off his jacket and his sweater, and a thin, light-blue t-shirt was all that covered his muscled torso. *Focus, Evie. You can objectify your husband in a few minutes.* "Your vows, and how you went out of your way to make the wedding perfect."

"You deserve perfect. It's what you give me, every day."

Hardly, but if Liam had taught her anything over the last year and a half together, it was that she didn't need to put herself down or make excuses. She looked at his face, so close to hers now, and smiled at the love written all over it. "We're good for each other, aren't we?"

"Hell, yeah. Without you, I'd be a miserable workaholic, and I'd have no clue how sexy a tool belt could be."

"So sexy." She pressed her lips against his, pausing before he could deepen the kiss. "You've made my world so much bigger and brighter, Liam. I love you."

With a satisfied, rumbling sound in his throat, he parted her lips with his, teasing her tongue to come out and play. She didn't need to be asked twice. She tugged his shirt up, fisting the fabric in one hand as she ran the other over his clenching abs.

Liam twisted both hands into her hair, which she'd worn loose so he could do exactly that, and held her in place as he kissed her slowly, thoroughly. With intent.

"We're all alone," he whispered roughly against her mouth.

"I know..." She arched her back, pressing their bodies together.

"I mean, we were alone last night. But—" He cut himself off, and she pulled him in tighter. He didn't need to feel badly for wanting to be just them for a few nights.

"But this time, the kids are four hours away and there's zero chance of being interrupted." Nipping at his lower lip, she pressed her mouth against his. Open and inviting.

His hands worked their way inside her shirt, finding her bra strap as he rolled his tongue against hers, sparking a fire in her core.

They needed to get naked. She needed his mouth on her, everywhere, and then it would be her turn to lick him all over. She couldn't wait.

Knocking at the door doused that plan with cold water.

Liam twisted them around, hiding her with his body so she could sort out her bra, and the fly on her jeans, which he'd somehow gotten open while she'd been grinding against him.

"Hey there," she heard a voice calling from the doorway.

———

LIAM SWALLOWED a frustrated groan and cleared his throat as he walked from the kitchen to the foyer area. "You must be Ryan Howard, Finn's brother. Liam McIntosh, nice to meet you."

The other man held out his hand, and Liam took it. He wasn't as dark as Finn, but you could see the family resemblance—they both looked like Irish heavy-weight boxers. *Country boys*, Evie would say with a smile when he teased her that she'd ended up with the skinny kid. Then she'd wrap herself around him and he'd carry her to the bedroom, and it wouldn't matter that he was more *swimmer's build* than *football player*.

"Just wanted to make sure you found everything okay," Ryan said. He nodded at Evie, who'd come to stand beside Liam. "Welcome to Pine Harbour."

"Thank you." She held out her hand. "We really appreciate all you did to set this up for us."

"If you need anything, I'm at the top of the lane."

Liam wrapped his arm around Evie's shoulders. "Finn mentioned a diner?"

"Yep. That's Mac's, in town. And Anne Minelli has a nice cafe, too. Go up to the highway, turn left, then it's the next left, a few minutes down the road. You'll see a sign."

"Thanks so much, man." *Now leave us alone so I can fuck my bride.*

Evie shook against his side, like she could read his mind, but she waited until the other man had nodded and let himself out before dissolving completely into laughter.

"What?" he grumbled as she flipped the lock on the door, then slowly walked down the length of windows, dropping the blinds on each one as she went.

"So much for not being interrupted," she said, a playful smile on her lips as she glanced back at him over her shoulder.

"We're not answering the door if he comes back." Liam prowled toward her.

"Leave him alone," Evie said, fisting the front of his shirt when he bumped into her, moving her back against the wall. "He's the one that lost his wife a couple months ago, remember? He probably wasn't even thinking about it being the first night of our honeymoon."

"He's a guy," Liam protested.

"He looked so sad," Evie whispered, brushing her lips against his jaw. "And lost."

Yeah, Liam hadn't seen any of that. "I'll take your word for it, sunshine. Now, where were we?"

She slid her hand down his body and stroked her palm over his pulsing erection, squeezing him through his now-too-tight jeans. "Right here."

His abs pulled tight as she undid his belt, then opened his fly. "Evie..."

"I love the way you say my name," she whispered. He fell forward, bracing his forearm on the wall by her head as she freed his cock. With his other hand, he clumsily worked at the button on her jeans, and as soon as her bare belly was free, he leaned in, pressing his throbbing length to her warm skin. She did most of the work to get them naked, because he was lost in the scent of her hair and the warmth of her body as he pinned her against the wall.

"I'm going to say it every day for the rest of our lives. Just like that, like I need you. Because I do," he said roughly, rocking his hips against her. "Your touch undoes me, Evie Calhoun. Your whispered words get under my skin and your little looks make me feel like a hundred feet tall."

"Oh, Liam," she whimpered, wrapping her arms around his neck as she pulled herself up his body. He could feel she was wet and ready for him, but he wanted to taste her first.

He started with her mouth. Eager tongue and sweet lips. He'd never get enough of kissing his wife. Then her neck, and her breasts, her nipples tightening under his tongue. Her belly, mostly flat again. He kissed her stretch marks and licked the faint outline of her muscles.

Settling on his knees, he lifted one of her legs onto his shoulder and leaned in, loving how she rocked her hips forward, offering her pussy to him. Trusting that he found every last inch of her beautiful and desirable and completely delicious.

She was wet, her folds glistening as he took in the beauty of her pussy. And that was his last truly coherent thought as he leaned in, covering her with his mouth. Loving her this way was primal and earthy. Her scent filled his head with urges to take her, ravish her hard and leave her full of his babies.

It was totally medieval, how much that turned him on. Before he'd met Evie, children had been an abstract *maybe someday* idea. Then she'd come with two already, and they'd made a third on their first night together.

He'd been rocked at first, but not for long. Because Evie having his babies? That just felt right.

Flattening his tongue, he licked through her swelling folds, from her slippery opening to her taut little clit, standing proud and ready for him to suck between his lips.

"Liam," she begged again, pulling at his hair, and he glanced up. "Now. I need you in me, now."

"Later, then," he muttered as he surged to his feet, picking her up as he braced his feet wide. After fitting them together and sliding deep inside her, he spread one palm against the wall and used the other arm to hold her bottom, but Evie did most of the work. She flexed her legs around his hips and used her arms over his shoulders to lift herself up a few inches, then sink back down.

The whole time, her gaze was glued to his face.

"You're so beautiful."

"You're drunk on sex," she laughed, gasping as he drove hard into her in response.

"I'm drunk on my wife."

Her eyes went all soft at that, and she licked her lips before leaning in to kiss him, little sipping kisses that deepened as they got closer to a mutual climax. Liam's balls pulled tight against his body and his cock thickened inside the tight sheath of her sex as she dragged herself up and down his cock, faster and harder with each rise.

She made these little moaning sounds into his mouth each time they slid back together, and as they ran together, he started snapping his hips, chasing that spot inside her that would push her over the edge.

Because as soon as she started coming around him, he was going to let himself loose, but she needed to get there first.

She always needed to come first.

Rule number one of worshiping your wife. Make her come first, and come often.

"Come with me," she gasped, her legs so tight

around him now that she was really just rocking her clit against the base of his cock.

"I'm there," he grunted, slamming into her once more, releasing his seed deep inside her as she clenched around him. The spasms pulled the rest of his orgasm out of him, and he closed his eyes, dropped his face to her neck.

Evie. His one-night stand, turned mother of his children, and now his wife.

He was the luckiest man in the world.

She thumped her head back against the wall, letting out a long sigh. "Wow."

"Mmmm."

"Keep doing that, and you're totally going to knock me up this trip."

He pressed his hips into her. "I hope so."

"Ready for another round of sleepless nights?" She wiggled her legs and he set her down. Hand in hand, they walked to the bathroom, looking for the shower.

He started it, then stepped back and held out his hand, gesturing for her to get in first. "I can't wait for more sleepless nights."

She laughed and pulled him in with her. "You're a crazy man, you know that?"

"Yep." He settled her under the steaming water, then followed the droplets down her body with his hands. "Seriously. I know it's not the life that everyone wants, but our family can be as big as you want it to be."

She leaned into his chest, hiding her face in his skin.

Wrapping his arms around her, he kissed the top of her head. "You okay?"

She nodded. "Better than okay."

"Can I wash your hair?"

She laughed and twisted around in his arms. "Okay, now it's official. I've died and gone to heaven." Glancing back over her shoulder, she grinned at him, lighting up his world yet again.

Liam pulled her back against his body. He never wanted to let her go. "That's exactly how I want you to feel, every day. Happy honeymoon, my wife."

THE END

Speaking of Pine Harbour, have you read Love in a Small Town, the first book in that series? Turn the page for an excerpt.

And have you read all the Wardham stories?

Between Then and Now - Carrie & Ian's story
What Once Was Perfect - Laney & Kyle's story
Where Their Hearts Collide - Karen & Paul's story
When They Weren't Looking - Evie & Liam's story
Beyond Love and Hate - Beth & Finn's story
No Time Like Forever - Chase & Mari's story
Perfect No Matter What - Laney & Kyle's wedding

Forever Begins with a Kiss - Chase & Mari's wedding

And coming soon

All That They Desire - Evan, Jess & Brent's story

Make sure you're on my mailing list to receive all the Wardham updates!
www.smarturl.it/ZoeYorkNewsletter

EXCERPT FROM LOVE IN A SMALL TOWN,
PINE HARBOUR #1

It was bad enough that after going through a very public divorce from the man Olivia still loved, she had to serve him breakfast four times a week. That she looked forward to those mornings...well, that wasn't great either. But Rafe worked two jobs and lived in a tiny one-room apartment. And the other option for eggs and bacon was his mother's café.

Liv shuddered at the thought of spending even one morning a week with her ex-mother-in-law. So she couldn't fault Rafe for keeping his regular stool at the diner she worked at, even if it didn't help the official party line held by all six hundred people in their small town of Pine Harbour—that their split had been her fault and Rafe was completely innocent.

The former point was true. The latter was not. Parsing the difference with the town busy-bodies was a futile effort though, so she let the whispers slide. They just added to the steaming pile of crap that was her life.

But the absolute worst was that today, Rafe had brought a date to breakfast.

And she'd serve him eggs and paste on a smile, but then she was calling a real estate agent. Whatever cosmic joke had made her fall in love with Rafe Minelli had delivered its final punch line.

He wasn't in uniform today—either of them—but he still looked achingly good. Faded blue jeans that she recognized from the irregular rip on one of his solid thighs. Old enough that she'd washed them many times. The denim would be soft, and when he turned around, his wallet would be clearly imprinted in his back right pocket. And even though she wanted to grab a butter knife and gouge his heart out, first she wanted one more look at his magnificent ass.

Because she was a glutton for punishment, and Rafe delivered in bucket loads. Tall, dark, and handsome didn't do him justice. Olivia grabbed a washcloth and wiped down the counter as she watched him guide his date to a booth under the window.

No! She wanted to shout. *You sit at the counter and ask me if it's been busy. I bug you that you need a haircut and we both remember that time I gave you a trim in the bathroom. How you slid your hands under my shirt and teased my nipples while I squealed for you to hold still.* The walk down memory lane cut sharper than usual because it wasn't shared. Even though she knew she needed to move on, let go of Rafe and start dating again, she wasn't prepared to see *him* do just that. And the pretty blonde woman sitting across from him twisting the shit out of a sugar packet was wearing one of his plaid shirts, so Olivia couldn't even pretend it was a breakfast meeting—not that Rafe would ever have business that needed to be discussed in a diner.

He was a full-time police officer and a part-time soldier. Had been a full-time son and a part-time husband, too. No room for a wife, definitely no room for a side job. No, this was definitely a morning-after-a-sleep-over breakfast and Olivia had to serve him fucking coffee. She wrenched the carafe from the warmer, grabbed two menus from under the counter, and pasted on her sweetest eat-shit-and-die smile before squaring her shoulders and approaching the couple.

"Coffee?"

They both nodded and Olivia silently lifted each of their white ceramic mugs and poured. For someone who just got laid, Rafe didn't look happy. His eyebrows were pulled together, hooding his gaze, and he had faint dark circles under his eyes. Maybe he was realizing just how awful a human being he was to bring...

"Do you need to see a menu, Natalie?" His voice sounded strained too. He dumped two creamers in his cup and stirred roughly.

Natalie, huh? Olivia swung her gaze to the other

woman. She looked nervous. Had he told her that he used to be married to their waitress? Used to wake her up with his tongue and his hands and his love, but not as often as he didn't—he'd have to be home for that—and now they pretended to be friends a few times a week?

"I'll just have some toast, please," she said quietly.

Rafe sighed. "Don't be silly." He looked up at Olivia, his dark brown eyes unreadable. "Two breakfast specials please, one with bacon, one with—" He broke off and turned back to Natalie. "Sausage? Ham?"

"Sausage, I guess. Look, I can just wait for my friend outside, we don't need to have breakfast."

"It's fine." He reached across the table and squeezed her hand before looking back at Olivia again. "Can I talk to you for a minute?"

"We're swamped," she said breezily, waving at the mostly empty diner. "I've got ketchup bottles to refill and napkins to stack, so—"

"One minute, Liv." He pushed out of the booth and towered over her. "In private."

He didn't wait for her to respond, stalking to the small office behind the washrooms like he owned the place. Well, he could wait. She had a job to do, even if it wasn't exciting or overly important.

"Natalie, is it? How did you want your eggs?" Rafe wanted his over-easy. At some point in the future, she'd forget all the stupid little things she knew about him. She hoped. Hadn't happened yet.

"Scrambled. And rye toast if you have it."

"Sure thing. Be right back." She went straight to the pass-through window, dinged the bell and tacked the order up on the carousel. Frank gave her a knowing look from his perch at the grill. "Shut up," she told her boss without malice. "I need five minutes."

"I'll holler if anyone comes in, I guess."

If anyone came in, they'd pour themselves a cup of coffee and wait. She wasn't worried. It wouldn't be the first time Pine Harbour had heard Rafe and Olivia Minelli have a knock-down, drag-out fight. Probably wouldn't be the last. Another reason she needed to leave. This couldn't be her future—petty jealousy and tension-filled terse conversations with her ex. She took a deep breath and shoved the office door open.

She was pissed, and he deserved it, but he didn't have time to deal with that right now. He held up his hand, cutting off whatever smart remark was about to slide out of her beautiful mouth. "It's not what you think."

"I think she's wearing your shirt." She dropped her head, like she didn't want to look at him, and her long brown ponytail fell over her shoulder. One of the sad side effects of not living with Olivia anymore—never seeing her hair down. He liked the ponytail because it was so her, practical and cute and sporty, but he loved the dark curtain of free-falling hair that he'd only seen in private. Now reserved for his fantasies, that image of Liv completely undone, tousled and sexy, was a favourite memory. Eyes blazing, the Olivia right in front of him would light him up if she knew what he was thinking about. "I think you know better than to bring her here, but you're more scared of your mother than you are of me, and fair enough. Your mom is frightening as all get out. And I know I have no right to care about what you do and who you do it with. I get that. So I will bite my tongue. But you don't get to summon me back here for a chat while your new girlfriend sits out there waiting for you. That's awful, Rafe. That's not *you*."

Wow, she went in a different direction than he'd expected. "Okay, hold up." He let out a sigh as his phone vibrated in his pocket. He yanked it out and swore under his breath at the call display screen. "Listen, I have to take this, but we're not done here."

She laughed, short and sharp and completely without humour. "Oh, we're definitely done here." She spun and jerked the door open, pausing in the doorway. "Your girlfriend takes her eggs scrambled, by the way."

She's not my anything, he wanted to yell, but that wasn't completely true. Natalie had been his distraction of the month the night before. He'd bought her a few drinks and let her sit on his lap. Played with the bare skin at her waist and enjoyed the way she smelled. They'd kissed, and more than once. But he walked her to her car at the end of the night of pool and pints at The Green Hedgehog in Lion's Head—Pine Harbour not being big enough for a pub of its own—only to discover that it wouldn't start. And her friend, who'd left with Matt Foster, wasn't answering the phone. Rafe knew he should call her a tow truck, but it was a long tow to Owen Sound, the small city the girls lived in, and that left the problem of how her girlfriend would get home the next day.

So he'd offered her his bed. Without him in it. Something Natalie had tried to persuade him to change his mind on, a totally fair move on her part. But he hadn't slept with anyone since Liv. Wasn't sure when and if he'd be able to. Unlike his wife, he'd meant his wedding vows when he'd sworn to love her forever. Liv leaving him didn't change that.

But just because he couldn't get over her didn't mean he shouldn't try. He *should* try, and once a month he let his buddies drag him to Lion's Head or Sauble Beach to get back in the game. This was the first time one of those pitiful attempts at a social life had played out in front of Liv, though. And he couldn't worry about that because Dean was blowing up his phone.

"What?"

"Good morning to you, too, sunshine. We got a problem."

"It's my day off, man."

"Operation Paper Cut has been bumped up. Inspector Wagner wants all available officers called in."

A major bust. There was only one answer. "Sleep first?"

"Yeah. Report at four this afternoon."

He hung up without saying goodbye. He'd be there. But first he needed to eat, then he had two women to sort out.

When he stepped back into the main space of the diner, Liv was quietly buttering toast at the counter and resolutely not looking in his direction. Natalie stared out the window. It wasn't her fault he was hung up on someone else, or that Pine Harbour was so small this was their only option for breakfast that didn't involve his mother.

Anne Minelli was only Italian by marriage, but she'd adopted her husband's culture completely, right down to happily becoming a caricature of an over-protective mother—and a nightmare of a mother-in-law to the only other woman who'd had the misfortune to marry into the Minelli clan.

Rafe wasn't the oldest son. That privilege fell to his older brother Zander, who'd gotten the hell out of Dodge at eighteen. Where Rafe and his younger brother Tom had enlisted in the local army reserve unit after high school, Zander had gone reg force and was currently stationed in Wainwright, Alberta. The only member of their family not in the military was the baby, his sister Dani, and that wasn't for lack of trying.

Speak of the devil. The door chimed and in she walked. Dressed in her navy paramedic uniform, she was so focused on Liv and the coffee pot that she didn't see him. Trailing behind her was his friend Ryan Howard, another EMS worker, who gave him a distracted nod as he checked something on his phone.

"Hey, sister-of-mine, can we get two coffees to go?" They even looked like sisters, Dani taller and lankier, Liv shorter and curvy in all the right places. Her endearment for his ex-wife was a punch in the gut reminder that even after the divorce Dani and Liv had remained close. Familiar bitterness set his jaw on edge and he turned away from watching them.

But he couldn't stop listening.

"Sure thing, baby girl. What's up, Ryan?"

The other man grunted something about a weekend road trip for his brother Finn's wedding. Rafe had heard a bit about it the week before at poker night. A four-hour drive south to a tiny town called Wardham.

Rafe hadn't asked too much about the trip because after his divorce, poker, hockey and work were the only safe subjects between him and Ryan. The Howards had been the only real couple friends he and Liv had, and while he and Ryan were still friendly, Lynn had taken Liv's side in the divorce in a big way. Which he didn't care about—most of the time, *he* was on Liv's side in this whole mess. She'd deserved more than he'd given her. But she hadn't given him a chance to make it right.

If you could have. Maybe not. But he'd deserved a fucking chance.

At the end of the day, that's why he'd filed for divorce. If she didn't want him, he wasn't going to beg. He'd held on to the last scraps of his dignity and moved out. He hadn't gone far—obviously—but he'd given her what she wanted.

Even though it killed him. Not for the first time, he wondered if he'd made a mistake asking her if she wanted a divorce—offering her that out he hadn't wanted her to take. He never expected her to say yes. That had gutted him.

He slid into the booth with a sigh.

"I'm sorry about all of this," Natalie said nervously. "Maybe you should have taken me to your friend's place last night instead."

And interrupt whatever fun Matt was having with her friend? Rafe wasn't going to force his own celibacy on others. "It's fine."

"Clearly." She toyed with her spoon, flipping it back and forth on the table. He wanted to take it away from her. Wanted her to drink her coffee and wait for her food and not stare at him like he'd hurt her feelings and she was hoping he'd suddenly see that and make it all better.

He had no clue how to do that. Not for his wife, not

for this stranger wearing his shirt. Definitely not for his mother, who hadn't really spoken to him in two years. "Listen, Natalie, if I lead you on..."

"You kissed me and invited me back to your place."

"Because you were stranded. It's not you, it's me. You're gorgeous. I'm just not available."

"Are you gay?"

He thought about saying yes, but Liv chose that moment to deliver their plates and he didn't want her to hear any of their conversation. *Genius move, coming here.* Instead of answering, he busied himself with salt and pepper and ketchup. By the time he looked up she was eating. *Just as well.*

Matt finally texted and confirmed he could drive the girls to their car and wait for a tow truck with them—and even better news, they were en route. Without a word, Rafe slid his phone across the Formica tabletop so Natalie could read it. Relief flitted across her face. He didn't wait for Liv to bring them a bill. Their breakfast would be exactly twice his usual. He left three times as much on the table and escorted his sort-of-but-not-really date out to the parking lot just as Matt roared up in his bright blue F-150.

Natalie hesitated when her friend opened the passenger door and gestured for her to get in. "About your shirt..."

"Don't worry about it."

"Maybe if they have another date, I can send it back with her."

Matt Foster rarely hooked up with the same woman more than once. He preferred to leave them with a happy smile after the first—and only—go round, before any attachment could form. The man managed to stay on this side of having a player reputation, and no doubt the next time he saw Natalie's friend, she'd squeal and give him a big sloppy kiss on the cheek. But that would be it for them. "Yeah. Maybe."

———

Rafe scuffed his boot in the hard pack dirt at the bottom of the diner steps. He'd paid. His guest was gone. He had no reason not to get in his own truck and head home for some much needed sleep.

He definitely had no explanation for jogging up the steps and stepping inside. Liv hadn't cleared his dishes yet, even though the place was now empty. Instead, she was tidying every other part of the space. Squaring off chairs around the tables in the middle of the room. Refilling napkins.

She reached over the counter for her damp rag, and he let himself have his fill of staring at her nipped-in waist and the flare of her hips. The memory of cupping her bottom as she slowly rode him in the middle of the night was bittersweet—one he never wanted to forget, and had desperately needed to get over.

His dick had other thoughts. Like closing the gap between them and pressing up against her, his front to her back. Hugging and kissing and making it all right.

But there was no magical cure for mismatched love. And anything less than that would just be a variation on disrespecting her. It was all that had held him back from suggesting something casual over the last twenty-four months. She deserved more than a furtive roll in the hay with her ex.

So instead of groping her or begging for sexual scraps, he forced himself to saunter to his table, grab his mug, and head for the coffee pot.

She knew he was there. She'd glanced at him in the mirrored panels over the pass-through. "Your girlfriend get off okay?"

He poured the hot, black liquid into his cup, grateful for the furious sloshing noise it provided. "I told you," he drawled slowly. "It's not what it looks like."

"It's none of my business."

"I'm always your business." In his chest, his heart thumped a little harder at the way her spine straightened when he said that. "I was Matt's wingman last night and her car wouldn't start at the end of the night. It was just easier to let her stay at my place."

"Let me put this another way," she said coldly, her back still to him. "I don't want to know."

"I slept on the couch." The words grated out of him, and he knew it probably sounded like he resented having to explain himself. Except he didn't. He'd come back inside to make sure she knew what had really happened. If he was gruff, that was more due to not knowing how the explanation would land. Doubt that it would be received as he hoped.

She whirled on him, eyes blazing and cheeks pink. "Do you think that makes you some sort of hero, Rafe? We're divorced. You're supposed to move on and date other people."

"I'm not supposed to do it in front of you."

She laughed, a sad, empty sound. "Hard to avoid that in a town of six hundred people."

"We were in Lion's Head, actually."

She held up her hand. "Still don't want to know."

He took a sip of coffee. All the things he wanted to say froze in his throat. *Give me a second chance. You look tired and gorgeous at the same time. Are you dating anyone?*

"I'm glad you're moving on," she said, her voice softening. "It's been...like time has frozen for us. And we're too young for that. I just don't want to see it."

He took a final swig of coffee and glared at her across the diner. Then he rinsed his cup in the sink and placed it in the dirty dishes bin before prowling around the counter and getting close enough to see the whites of her eyes as she lifted her brow in surprise.

"I'm not moving on." He matched her slow, quiet

tone. They'd done enough yelling, him and Liv. He reached out and put his hands on her hips. She felt different, like maybe she'd lost some weight there. "Are you eating enough?"

"What?" She pushed hard against his chest, but he wasn't going to be moved. "Rafe, give me some space."

"Give me a minute, then I'll back off. Give me a minute to show you just how much I haven't *moved on*, Liv."

Her breath caught in her throat and a tear started to form in the corner of her eye. *Damn.*

"No, baby, please don't cry." His voice cracked and he didn't care. He hauled her tight against him and buried his face in her hair. Still the same shampoo.

"We have to stop doing this," she said into his shirt with a hiccup.

I'm never going to stop. I'm never going to let you go. "I can't, baby. I lo—"

"No." She struggled again and he eased his grip to give her some space. "No. You can't say that." She wiped her eyes and sniffed, then waved her hands between their bodies. "You need to stop coming in here. Alone. With people. Mac's is now off-limits to you."

OTHER SERIES BY ZOE YORK

If you've enjoyed Wardham, you might want to visit **Pine Harbour** (small town military romance just a few hours north of Wardham), **Camp Firefly Falls** (sexy rom coms at an adult summer camp), as well as the Navy SEALs in **SEALs Undone** and **ASSIGNMENT: Caribbean Nights**.

And coming in 2019...the last book in the Wardham series, All That They Desire, which will segue into a brand-new series set in the same area, **Whisper Beach**. Wardham's getting even sexier!

Visit my website and join my mailing list to be the first to hear about new books!

ACKNOWLEDGEMENTS

SO many people to thank on this book. Sadie Haller, a wonderful author and friend, who was my first reader and flagged all the things. All of them. Oh my, the comma offences you were saved from seeing!

Dana Waganer, the loveliest and most easygoing proofreader ever.

All my readers who wanted an epilogue for Evie and Liam's story, and were willing to wait a year for it.

The Chatzy Crew for all the writing sprints.

My husband, who made me late-night fires, drove kids to school and daycare, literally vacuumed around me as I pounded away at the keys, and cooked all the food we ate this month. And also for marrying me a billion years ago, so I could have the perfect wedding inspiration for this book.

My kids, for thinking that curling up next to me on the couch was cool.

The lovely Ruth Hay, who wrote her first book long before I did, and who could teach me a million things about being a reader and a writer and a true book fan.

And finally, Lee Brice and Maroon 5, for providing the very limited soundtrack of two (perfect) songs for this story. My iTunes account is slightly shocked at the number of repeats on "I Don't Dance" and "Sugar".

ABOUT THE AUTHOR

Zoe York lives in London, Ontario with her young family. She's currently chugging Americanos, wiping sticky fingers, and dreaming of heroes in and out of uniform.

Connect with Zoe:
www.zoeyork.com
zoeyorkwrites@gmail.com

BE A WARDHAM AMBASSADOR

I'd love to have you join my Facebook reader group!
Click on the link, or search "Wardham Ambassadors"
on Facebook.